THE
CENTER
OF THE
WHEEL

To Penny,
I hope this
book brings smile
and blessings.
Robert Hudson

THE
CENTER
OF THE
WHEEL

Robert Hudson

ENLIGHTENED QUEST PUBLISHING
Birmingham, Alabama
1998

Enlightened Quest Publishing
P. O. Box 11692
Birmingham, Alabama 35202

ISBN: 0-9660823-0-3
LCCN: 97-094508

This is a work of fiction. Names, characters, places, and incidents are either the product of the author's imagination or are used fictitiously.

Cover design and illustration by Vicki Schenck-Atha

Manufactured in the United States of America
10 9 8 7 6 5 4 3 2 1

Attention Organizations and Groups:
There are discounts available on bulk purchases of this book when used for purposes of education, fund raising, etc. Also, other fund raising opportunities using book excerpts may be possible.

For information, please write to:
Robert Hudson,
c/o Enlightened Quest Publishing,
P.O. Box 11692,
Birmingham, Alabama 35202.

Within each of us there is a voice or feeling
that guides us as we make our way through life.
We don't know the origin of this guide.
We're not sure what it is or what to call it.
Nevertheless it is there,
speaking to us through our thoughts, feelings,
and physical sensations.
Some call it the voice of God;
others call it intuition.
It has many names.

Acknowledgements

I want to offer my sincere appreciation to all those who directly or indirectly influenced the creation of this book.

I want to thank and recognize the many people who helped in the editing process: Marjorie Jones, Joy Resor, Trudie Hudson, James Redfield, Carol Grizzle, Alison Grizzle, Diane Brasher, Alyce Head, Lulu Richardson, Kyle Strange, Dan Warren, Rusty Hudson, Gretchen Hudson, Tommy Morris, Cathy Wehrenberg, Jacquelyn Davis-Fowler, Sarah Resor, Larry Hampton, Les Ellis, Cindy Walchli, Jerry and Jane Bartholow, Robin Kaylor, Sue Kuechenmeister, Barbara Booth, Jonell Comegys, Nancy Wasson, Cindy Ponder, Larry Hanson, Jeff Thornton, Jean Ellis, Dale and Idong Ruffin, Kathy Dawson, and Sherry Sterling.

I want to express my sincere gratitude to James Redfield. It was my experience in assisting him in the creation of *The Celestine Prophecy* that motivated me to write *The Center of the Wheel*.

I also acknowledge the inspiration and guidance that I've received from my favorite writers: Hermann Hesse, Charlotte Joko Beck, Dan Millman, and Richard Bach.

And I want to give a special thanks to my wife, Trudie Hudson and my friend, Joy Resor for their patience and support throughout this whole project.

Author's Note

Life can be wonderful; it can also be harsh and can feel over-whelming at times. It is during these difficult times that I am reminded how much we need each other and how lonely and painful life can be.

The Center of the Wheel is my way of giving back some of what I have received. It is my way of saying thanks to the many people, friends and family, who have celebrated with me in the good times and who have helped me make it through the hard times.

My favorite books have always been the ones that make me smile as well as make me think. I hope *The Center of the Wheel* is such a book for you, and that you get as much from reading it as I did from writing it.

Contents

It has been said,

  "When the student is ready, the teacher will appear."

1 Struggling to Understand

Graduation day had arrived at last. I sat listening to the speeches, inwardly restless. The folding chairs sitting on the south lawn of the seminary were uncomfortable, and the speeches themselves seemed to me falsely grandiose, heightening my disquiet. Certain words occurred repeatedly: beginnings, opportunity, commencement, excitement, inception, responsibility, leadership. Was I the only one who felt uninspired? The words sounded lack-luster to me, as though the speakers were reading pages from the dictionary or *Roget's Thesaurus*.

I glanced around at some of my classmates. They all seemed to be paying close attention to the speaker at the podium, with eyes forward, seemingly riveted. Most of them had people present: parents, spouses, fiancés, siblings. I was alone. My mother, brother, and sister weren't able to come, and my father had died when I was young.

Wearing cap and gown in the heat of the Kentucky sun at the end of May added to my discomfort. I found myself squirming. Paul, my roommate, was sitting behind me. He tapped my back, whispering, "David, are you okay?" I nodded "yes" and tried harder to be still. I was probably disturbing him with my wiggling.

When the ceremonies ended, my classmates came one by one to shake hands and exchange congratulations. Paul and I hugged self-consciously. He said, "I'm off to Tennessee, to my new church. Wish me well, Dave."

"You know I wish you the best," I told him. "You'll do great. They're lucky to have you."

Then it was goodbye.

Later, back in our room, I found myself feeling even more alone. With all of Paul's stuff gone, the place looked empty – as empty as I felt. As I folded my pants and shirts and put them in my suitcase, I thought back to Paul asking if I was okay. I wondered how he would have reacted if I had said: "No, nothing's okay. For starters, I don't have a job. Besides, I'm not sure that I haven't wasted my time here."

Possibly, I was the only graduate in that situation. Unlike most seminarians, I hadn't entered the seminary to become a minister. Instead, my hope was to find answers.

I sat down on what used to be Paul's bed. I was dejected. I felt totally alone and miserable. Images of my mom and dad flooded my mind. Tears welled up in my eyes as I thought back to the day of my father's death, the day my search for answers had begun.

I remembered that day as if it were today, even though I was only five when it happened. I could feel the anguish and rage stirring up in me as I flashed back, reliving the whole experience.

My mother had sent me to stay with friends for a while because my father was sick and needed extra attention. One week passed. Two weeks passed, and I was still staying with friends. I began to wonder if something was wrong.

When my mother and brother came to pick me up, the strained expressions on their faces validated my fears. Something *was* wrong – something was *terribly* wrong.

By the time we arrived at home, my stomach was churning. I couldn't put it into words, but a terrible feeling had come over me. The house felt empty as I stepped through the front door. I sensed what was missing, and though I didn't want to confirm what I already knew was true, I slowly walked down the hall to my father's room. He wasn't there. His bed was empty, and he was gone.

I didn't ask any questions; in fact, I didn't say anything to anyone. I grabbed "Monk" and "Bully Bear," two of my stuffed animal friends, and I headed to the backyard to get away from the terrible reality before me. It was too awful, and I couldn't face it, at least not yet.

That evening, when I could avoid the truth no longer, it finally hit me, "My daddy's gone. He's dead." No one had to tell me. No one had to explain. I just knew. He was gone forever. Still, I couldn't understand why such a dreadful thing had happened. I had been a "good boy," or at least I thought I had. What had I done to deserve this?

The fear and confusion inside of me turned into rage, rage at God. I went to the living room, where my mother was sitting, and with tears of grief and anger streaming down my face, I shouted, "I hate God! I hate God for taking my daddy away!"

My mother pulled me to her, and through her own sobs she said, "It will be okay. It will be okay." But I knew better; it was not okay. Something was wrong in such a world where a little boy's father could be taken away from him, stolen from him without even an opportunity to say goodbye. Something was wrong in such a world where there was supposed to be a loving God, a God that I had prayed to every night, saying, "God protect Mommy, Daddy, Frank, and Jenny." But God did not protect them; instead, He took my daddy away. Something was wrong, and I knew it. The wrongness screamed inside me. I cried harder, heaving and shaking, feeling that my insides were being torn from me.

After I calmed down, my mother tried to explain why things had happened as they did. She said, "God knew that your daddy was very sick and that he was hurting awfully bad. God took your daddy so he wouldn't have to hurt anymore. Now, he's in heaven, and all of his pain is gone." But my mother's explanation did not make a whole lot of sense to me. If God was as powerful and as great as everyone said, then why didn't He heal my dad? Why would God take a five year old's dad away?

Now twenty-one years later, even after three years of seminary, I had the same questions and still no answers.

It took me another hour to finish packing. Then I loaded

boxes, suitcases, guitar, and stereo into my old Duster and headed down the road toward home. It was a long anxious trip. My mind refused to focus on anything except that I was jobless. Again and again, I reviewed the process of my job search, reliving the hours I had put into perfecting my resumé. I had done everything I had known to do. My undergraduate degree was in education, and what I wanted to do was teach. My brother, who taught in Georgia, had encouraged me to apply all over. He said teaching positions were becoming harder and harder to come by. I had sent resumés to the major school systems in three states.

After what seemed like forever, I finally crossed the Georgia state line and ninety minutes later I pulled into Mom's driveway. She greeted me with a hug and a kiss, and there was a hot apple pie waiting for me on the stove. Thoughts of not having a job briefly faded away as I took comfort in being back home.

The next day, the comfort of home slowly wore off, and the reality of my situation gradually reappeared, taking hold of my mind. Mom sensed the change in my demeanor and questioned what was wrong. I didn't want to worry her and pretended it was nothing.

"Oh, I'm just tired. It's been a long week," I told her.

I sat around the house the next few days, idle, anxious, and frustrated. After a while, I was no longer able to get by with saying that nothing was wrong. Finally I told Mom my problem. She suggested that I send out more resumés. And though I knew it was too late in the year to help me get a teaching position for the fall, I took her advice. It was better than just sitting around feeling helpless.

I also began looking for a temporary job, one that could get me by until I could find somewhere to teach. However, even a temporary job was difficult to come by. We lived in a small town and there just wasn't anything available.

That's how I spent the summer, looking for work and sending out more and more resumés. Every afternoon after a fruitless day of job hunting, I went to the mailbox hoping for good news. But by early July, I had nothing but turn downs. I felt disheartened. Frustration was eating at me. All of those years of school and I couldn't even find a job.

I started joining some of my old friends for beer in the evenings. I needed an escape. Though I knew alcohol wasn't the answer, my self-esteem was at an all-time low and life seemed easier and not so depressing after a couple of beers.

Then, toward the end of July, when I'd all but given up hope of finding a teaching position for the coming year, the phone rang. It was the coordinator of a school in Birmingham, Alabama. I had been interviewed there in the spring, but someone else had gotten the job. Now, another position had come open. I had wanted to stay in Georgia, but since I hadn't received any other offers, I accepted the position with little hesitation. Besides, my younger sister, Jenny, lived in Birmingham and it would be great to see her and her son, Alex, more often. When I called to let her know the news, she was elated, insisting that I stay with her until I found a place of my own.

*   *   *

I arrived in Birmingham at one o'clock on a hot, muggy August afternoon, anxious and excited, yet full of mixed feelings about moving and taking on my first real job. Jenny was not expecting me until later in the afternoon, so no one was home when I arrived. Not having a key, I went to the trunk of my car, pulled out my guitar, a pad, and a pencil, and took a seat on one of the redwood rockers on her front porch.

Jenny had done well for herself and Alex since her divorce, and on a social worker's salary no less. She lived at the end of a cul-de-sac in what seemed to be a normal, family-oriented neighborhood. Children played fearlessly up and down the street.

As I picked at my guitar, I found myself drifting into a fantasy world. One after another, thousands of thoughts and images passed through my mind. There was no pattern that I could see, just random thoughts. One second I was admiring Jenny's house, blue with white trim,… her freshly painted white porch, and the next instant anxious thoughts about my new job were making their way through my consciousness... "Can I do this job?... Will the kids like me?..." Then there was another shift of thoughts and images... "This rocker sure is comfortable... Jenny has put a lot of work into her yard... Her geraniums are beautiful... If I ever buy a house, I'm going to plant a few crape myrtles like these..." On and on the thoughts presented themselves.

Every once in a while, someone would pass by and say, "Hello," waking me from my reverie... Then back inside I would drift, one thought passing after another... "The people here seem friendly enough... Maybe this won't be a bad place to live, after all..." on and on, image after image.

Though the humidity was stifling, it was a wonderful day. The sky was a bright blue, and there were wisps of white clouds scattered here and there across the horizon. Before I knew it, I had drifted deep into myself, almost asleep, yet not quite.

Suddenly, there were footsteps on the porch. My eyes popped wide open. To my surprise, there was my Granddad standing on the porch in front of me. I rubbed my eyes and looked again. It *was* my grandfather. I'd always been told I resembled him. We were of average size and build, and we had reddish brown hair. His, at the temples, was now white giving him a distinguished appearance. I had a mustache while Granddad had a well trimmed beard with white streaks in it.

"Yep, it's me," he said with a chuckle.

"Where'd you come from?" I asked. I shook my head trying to gather my wits.

"North Carolina, of course," he replied nonchalantly.

"I know that. I mean, I didn't hear you walk up."

"I just kind of popped in, you know, magic like." His eyes, blue like mine, sparkled with amusement.

"No, really. What are you doing here?" I asked.

"Now, is that any way to greet someone you haven't seen for almost three years? Give me a hug."

I put my guitar aside, stood up and hugged Granddad. He

patted me on the back, and said, "It's good to see you. What'cha been up to? You done with all that *schoolin'* yet? You any wiser?"

It always tickled me when Granddad used southern verbiage, like "What'cha been up to?" or "schoolin'." Though he had lived all over the U.S., he had grown up in the south, and he was quite comfortable with southern language, sprinkling his speech with it now and then.

"Yeah, I've finished my *schoolin'*," I said, parroting his accent as best I could, "but I'm not sure what good it's done me. I don't feel a bit wiser. I still have a lot of learning to do, I'm afraid."

"I've a feeling there's a story beneath that statement," he said, virtually reading my mind.

"Not much of one," I replied, partially wanting to spill my guts, yet hesitant to do so. Granddad and I had never really conversed on a serious level. Our relationship was built on humor and horseplay.

"I'd like to hear it, if you're willing to tell it," he said, and then he waited patiently, as I considered his offer.

For the next thirty minutes or so, I told Granddad about my struggles. I told him about the stress, anxiety, and depression I had experienced over the summer when it didn't appear that I was going to find a job. I told him about my endless search to understand life and how college and seminary had done little or nothing to help me answer the myriad questions I had accumulated over the years.

While I was speaking, Granddad sat silently, listening to everything I said. Occasionally he nodded and I sensed the wisdom and empathy of one who had been there.

The longer I spoke the more aware I became that Granddad had changed. There was something different about him, but I couldn't quite name it. There was a peacefulness that I hadn't been aware of before. There seemed to be an aura of serenity surrounding him. He had always had a twinkle in his eye, and there had been a hint of mischief, too, but now his eyes seemed to have a soothing quality as well.

Granddad had always been different – unconventional and mysterious, yet down to earth. He lived in the foothills of North Carolina and spent much of his time in the mountains. He had never chosen to live life as others did. Granddad did things his own way. He had a small truck, but he rarely used it. He chose to walk, instead. He said he didn't go places just to get there but also to enjoy the trip – to stop and look at the flowers, pet the dogs, and talk with everyone along the way. Those things were not possible to do from the cab of a truck.

His life moved at a slower pace than everyone else's. He always had time for leisurely talks with anyone who happened along his path. Granddad loved people, and he liked to be of service to others. He was always cutting grass or raking leaves for people who couldn't do it for themselves. He liked to volunteer wherever he could. But he never cared much for working for money. He said that it didn't take much money to live, if one lived simply.

Gardening was another of his favorite things. Granddad said that having his hands in the dirt was therapy to him; it helped him feel grounded and one with the earth. His yard in North Carolina abounded with flowers virtually all year long. He grew many of his own vegetables, too, and he clearly had a way with tomatoes. His tomatoes made the best tomato and mayonnaise sandwiches I'd ever tasted.

Even though Granddad was an excellent gardener, in my opinion his expertise lay elsewhere. He was the best storyteller around. I could listen to him spin yarns all day and all night. He sometimes jumped up in the middle of a story to act as one of the characters. His eyes smiled mischievously when he was telling a tale. Other times, he might grab a pad and pencil to draw a quick sketch of a character.

Sometimes he seemed like an overgrown, elderly child. I can remember his pretending to be a wild animal, chasing my cousins and me through the house. I called him "Gorilla Gator" when I was young because that was the most fearsome wild animal name I could think of. When he caught us, he would tickle us, but never too much as some people do, and we would wiggle and scream with delight. After wrestling with us for a spell, he would fall to the ground as if exhausted. He would lie there a few seconds and then get up and start chasing us all over again. We loved it, and we loved him.

It had been close to three years since I had seen Granddad. Right after Grandma's death, he had taken a trip to the Orient and had stayed there longer than anyone in the family had expected. I'd heard he had returned, and now, suddenly, here he was standing in front of me. What was he doing here?

"Granddad, what are you doing here in Alabama?"

"I live here," he replied.

"I'm serious."

"I'm serious, too. I moved here about a week ago. I live right around the corner," he said, pointing.

"Does Jenny know?"

"Yeah."

"I wonder why she didn't tell me you were here. We just talked last night."

"I told her not to. I wanted it to be a surprise."

"Well, it certainly is!"

"I know. The look on your face was priceless," he replied grinning.

"But Granddad, what are you doing here? Really? Why would you up and move to Birmingham?"

"I don't really know how to explain it," he said, and then he paused for a few seconds before continuing. "Have you ever just felt like you needed to do something, but you didn't know why?"

"You mean like a hunch? Like intuition?"

"Exactly. Well, I had a hunch that I needed to move here, so I did."

"But for what reason?" I asked.

"That's not entirely clear yet, but I have no doubt that this is where I need to be. I can feel it in my gut."

"So you moved to Birmingham because of a feeling?" I asked in disbelief.

"Well yes,… but in a way, it's more than that."

"You must have a lot of faith in your intuition to move because it said to."

"David, I've lived a long life. I've followed my gut feelings some of the time, and other times I haven't. Every time that I haven't followed them, I've regretted it. I go with my gut all of the time now."

"That's kind of dangerous, isn't it? What if it told you to do something crazy, like kill somebody?"

"I wondered the same thing, at first. But I've found that my gut is consistently loving and compassionate, and the more I trust it, the more loving I become."

"Yeah, but some people hear voices and have inner yearnings that tell them to hurt people," I insisted.

"You're right, but if someone listens inside long enough, they will begin to know the difference between their gut and all of the other thoughts and feelings they might have. Another name for your gut is your true self. I see it as that part of you connected with all that is. It would never lead you to harm someone. It's not afraid of anything, and it never feels threatened or offended so it has no need to attack or defend. Your true self knows that we are eternal beings and that fear is just a hindrance most of the time. It's much wiser than one's conscious self and never gets all caught up in the mess of life. I believe that it's leading us toward health and wholeness. And when I listen to it, I get a sense of peace."

"Granddad, when you say that you feel it in your gut, what do you mean? Do you really feel it in your stomach?"

"Yeah, I feel it right here," he said, putting his hand on the upper part of his stomach.

"That's the main place I feel it, too... But sometimes, it's like I feel it all over my body. Do you ever feel it that way?" I asked.

"I think I know what you mean, because at times the feeling is so strong that I'm aware of it in my back and shoulders as well," he replied.

"And when you say 'feeling,' what do you mean? What's it like?"

"It's a sense of knowing," said Granddad. "There is a surety and confidence I feel. For example, when I think of two options, one of them feels shaky, but the other has a strong feel about it. And it's not really part of my thought process at all; it's more of a subjective, almost other worldly feeling. Kind of a sixth sense."

I nodded. "I just wanted to make sure we were talking about the same thing. I have those same kinds of intuitions, but I've never really thought of trusting them completely. I like to have more control than that. You know what I mean? I like to think things through and feel I am making the most logical, best decision after weighing my options."

"That's all right, as long as that works for you," he replied. "I've never been very successful with that approach myself. I always end up anxious and stressed out. Too much pressure."

"Yeah, that happens to me, too. I think it's because I'm a perfectionist."

Granddad smiled at that. "Perfectionism runs deep in our family. Like a disease."

That startled me. A disease? I'd always thought my striving for perfection was a plus.

Granddad went on, "When I was young, perfectionism virtually ran my life. It created a lot of anxiety and needless worry. It wasn't until I got focused and found out who I was, that I had some control over it. Now, I guess I'm a recovering perfectionist," he said with a grin. "I don't know that it will ever go away, but at least it's not in control anymore."

I laughed. "Recovering, huh,… How did you manage that?"

"Well, I guess we're all recovering from one neurosis or another. I really didn't have much choice in the matter. The neurosis finally quit paying off. Trying to be perfect made me miserable. My life began to feel worthless. I had spent my whole life trying to please and impress others, thinking that the better I was, the more love I'd receive. But I finally realized that it didn't work that way."

He kept surprising me. "What did you do to change?" I asked, becoming more and more interested in the direction he was heading.

"It wasn't until I met your grandmother that I started to

change. She was amazing, simply amazing. She just lived life, enjoying each and every moment. Seizing the day was easy for her. I still don't know what she saw in me. She could have had any boy around, but she chose me. Your Grandma had the ability to see past my faults and accept me just as I was, the good and the bad."

Listening to Granddad talk about Grandma was kind of neat. I hadn't heard many stories of their early days together. Usually when Granddad told tales, they were about his childhood.

"Once I experienced her acceptance of me," he continued, "I was better able to accept myself, and slowly the need for perfection seemed to fade. It didn't leave all at once, however. Twenty years of bad habits don't leave without a struggle. There was a lot of negativity within me, and the deeper I looked, the more mess I found."

While Granddad spoke, my mind searched for times that people had accepted me just as I was, "the good and the bad." My mother had always accepted me, but it wasn't until I was in my twenties that anyone other than my mom had really accepted me for who I was. I hadn't realized it before, but Granddad was right. The acceptance that I had received had been a significant factor in my starting to accept myself.

Granddad continued, "Yep, your grandmother gave me one of the greatest gifts anyone can give a person. She helped me to learn to love and accept myself. But after I began to accept myself, other challenges arose. All of a sudden, my self became a mystery to me. I had no idea who I really was. It didn't make sense to me that I could be loving one minute and hateful the next, full of purpose and direction one day, and then the next, totally lost. I was full of contradictions. I began to read every self-help book available to find some clue about who I was."

He had done it again – surprised me. "*You?... You* were unsure of who you were?" I had trouble accepting that idea.

He put his hand on my shoulder briefly and nodded. "Oh, yes! I was lost – not sure about much of anything... But the reading helped. And what I found was that as my awareness increased, two selves emerged. One was the self that I had acquired growing up. It was the anxious, worried part of me that was always striving to achieve and to establish a safe, secure life. The other 'me' or 'self' was totally secure and content. It seemed confident and unaffected by things around me."

I explored within. I, too, had more than one self. But as I looked, I couldn't narrow it down to two like Granddad had done.

I heard Granddad say, "The anxious part of me had many personalities. Each one functioned like a robot that had been programed by a society of neurotics that didn't have a clue about what life was really about. My perfectionism, along with other neurotic tendencies that plagued my life, resided in some of those misguided programs. There was a 'hero' program that wanted everyone to think I was great. It dreamed of saving a beautiful princess and living happily ever after. It believed that being great would make people love me. There was a 'be good' section, a 'be smart' section, and a 'be unusually gifted' section. The deeper I looked, the more different kinds of 'me' emerged. I kept peeling away layers upon layers of myself that were me, yet in a sense weren't the 'real' me."

The longer Granddad spoke, the more of me I heard in his words. In many ways, he was describing my life. I, too, had spent much of my life as a people pleaser who thought the more perfect I was the more love I would receive. I had even had the same dream of saving a beautiful woman from harm, marrying her, and living happily ever after. But Granddad had found himself, and I hadn't found the real me. I had been busy striving for success, busy trying to figure life out, but I wasn't even close to figuring out who I was.

"Granddad, tell me more about what you did to find your true self."

"Here, I'll show you something I did," he said, as he reached for my notebook which was lying in a nearby chair. "May I write on this?" he asked.

"Sure," I replied.

In my notebook, he drew what appeared to be a dart board or a target of some kind. He said, "Think of life as a target with a bull's-eye for its center. One of the first steps in figuring out who you are is to find out what belongs in the center of your target, what your priorities are, and what's important to you. When I was young, I wanted it all. I wasn't focused, so I kept scattering my energy in different directions. It wasn't until I narrowed things down and figured out what was important to me that life became less confusing. Once I knew what fit in my bull's-eye, I knew better how to use my time and energy."

Just then, Jenny and Alex pulled into the driveway.

"I guess we'll have to continue this conversation later," said Granddad and then he asked, "What'cha doin' tomorrow?"

"Not much," I replied. "I was just planning to hang out here. I need to look for a new car and an apartment, but not tomorrow."

"Well, why don't you come over and help me clean out my garage? We can talk some while we work. It probably won't take us more than a couple of hours. What do you think?"

"Sounds good to me. I'd like to talk some more. How about if I come over after breakfast?"

"That'd be fine," he replied.

Alex ran up the steps screaming, "Uncle David! Uncle David!"

"Hey there, buddy," I said, "Let me give you a hug."

I squatted and Alex wrapped his little, four-year-old arms around my neck.

"You want to play cars with me, Uncle David?"

"I sure do," I replied, "but let me say 'Hi' to your mom and talk with her a second first. Okay?"

"Okay. I'll go get my cars," said Alex. He ran to the front door and anxiously waited for his mother to unlock it so he could get in.

After unlocking the door, Jenny came over, gave me a hug and said, "Well, I see you've already found our little surprise."

"I wish you could have seen his face," Granddad chimed in.

"Y'all got me," I admitted.

They laughed, and Jenny ushered us inside. "How long have you been here? I didn't think you were coming until this evening."

"I wasn't, but I decided to come early."

"Okay, Uncle David, I'm back," cried Alex, entering the room–two cases of miniature cars under his arms. "You can have first pick, but let me have the dump truck. It's my favorite."

Within minutes Alex, Granddad, and I had chosen our cars and had them spread all over Jenny's living room floor. Her living room rug, with its alternating colored rings, created a perfect layout for playing cars. We used the different hued rings as roads, and the center section under the coffee table as a garage.

We played cars and talked for more than an hour before Granddad said he needed to be going. I walked him out.

As we strolled through Jenny's front yard, Granddad gave me directions to his house. We said goodbye, and he headed on his way. I watched him walk down the street for a few seconds and then went to the trunk of my car to retrieve some of my things. That's when the strangest thing happened. After unlocking my trunk, I glanced again, in Granddad's direction, and he wasn't there. He was gone! I stepped out from behind my car for a better view; he simply was nowhere in sight. I surveyed the area, but I couldn't see anywhere for him to be hiding, and why would he have been hiding anyway? He was gone. It was as if he had vanished into thin air.

Perplexed, I walked back to my car shaking my head. The thought of Granddad disappearing was absurd. There had to be a logical explanation, but I couldn't think of one, so I just let it go, grabbed my suitcase, closed the trunk, and headed to the house.

Alex continued to play cars until supper, while Jenny and I talked about old times. About nine o'clock, Jenny put Alex to bed, and a short time later we went to bed ourselves.

It had been a long day, and I was pretty wiped out. But when I lay down, I couldn't sleep. I lay awake, looking at the night sky through the window, as I thought about the days to come.

I was twenty-six years old, but it seemed as though my life was just beginning. The excitement about moving to a new city, getting my first apartment, and beginning my first real job was almost more than I could bear. I'd spent twelve… sixteen… twenty years in school, and finally, I was going to be able to use some of what I had learned. Though my future was a mystery,

I felt ready to experience it. The thought of living a normal life without research papers and tests seemed like heaven to me.

One of my college professors had said, "The secret to life is finding something you love to do and then finding someone who's willing to pay you to do it." It wouldn't be long until I found out if he was right.

As I lay there, my thoughts began to move in many directions. I was in a new place with new adventures ahead. Considering all that was before me, I decided that a talk with God was in order, which was an unusual thing for me to do. Prayer hadn't really been a big part of my life since my dad's death. Besides, God was supposed to know everything, anyway, so why bore Him by telling Him things He already knew? But that night, probably because I was a bit fearful about stepping into a whole new life, I felt like talking with Him. It wasn't exactly a prayer, really. It was more of a chat. I just spoke to Him as if I were talking with someone sitting right next to me.

> God, as you know, I don't talk with you very often. But you know my heart. You know that I'm twenty-six years old, and that I've got my whole life before me. You know that I want to live as you would want me to live, but you also know that sometimes I don't know exactly what it is that you want me to do. Please help me find my way.
>
> Also, God, I don't know if you want me to meet a woman in Birmingham or not. I'd like to meet one, but mostly God, I want what you want.
>
> If you do want me to meet one and I have any say in the matter, this is what I would like: I want a little blond, about five foot two inches tall with blue eyes. I would like us to be able to communicate easily, for her to be passionate, and for us to have lots of fun together. I also would like her to know how to play golf and the guitar. But mostly God, as I said before, I want what you want. Thy will be done. Amen.

I felt a little silly making such a request. God was not a cosmic bellhop or a divine matchmaker in charge of a cosmic dating game. But it was enjoyable saying the prayer nonetheless and laughing at the absurdity of it afterwards.

I fell asleep thinking about Granddad and the things he had said to me earlier in the day. The next thing I knew, I was in the midst of a dream, walking along a path beside a crystal stream. The water was flowing ever so gently over the rocks and into itself. The peacefulness of the water, with its fluidity and softness, was comforting to me. As I gazed into the stream, I lost my shape and became the water, fluid and flexible, resisting nothing, constantly trusting the path of the stream. There was no judgment in me, only experience. There was no striving, just awareness of the moment. Nowhere to go, nothing to do, but flow in the oneness of the stream.

My oneness with the water seemed endless, but then I was myself again, sitting on the grassy bank beside the crystal stream amid thousands and thousands of beautiful flowers. Rich colors and aromas enveloped me – lavender, turquoise, and rose. My eyes were dazzled; the scene filled me with awe.

I could have stayed beside the stream forever, but something within called me to leave. My path led elsewhere. A forest, dark and green, rose up before me. At its edge stood three figures dressed in glowing white gowns. The man in the center had long dark hair and a beard. He looked like Jesus, or at least, as I always thought Jesus might look based on the pictures of him I had seen in church. The man on the left looked Asian, and I thought to myself, maybe he was supposed to be the Buddha. And then I noticed the last man was my Granddad. What was he doing with Jesus and the Buddha? The three men appeared to be reading from a large, golden book that glittered and shone. The book appeared to be full of light, and it seemed that the dark haired man was writing in the book.

"Hello," I yelled, but they didn't look up or answer. Instead, they turned and walked into the forest. I screamed, "Granddad, wait," and I ran to catch them, but they seemed to move farther away. Finally, tiring out, I stopped running and started to walk.

It was then that the three men appeared again, standing together before a giant grayish-brown, stone wall. "Granddad," I yelled, and the three men looked up at me. Then they turned and walked right through the wall, as if it were not even there. I ran to the wall and found it to be as solid as it looked. It was taller than the trees, and to the left and right it went on endlessly. I had no idea how they had walked through it.

At a loss for what to do, I sat down to think. The wall was blocking my path, and I knew no way around it. The longer I pondered my situation, the more frustrated I became. Out of frustration, I began to hit the wall, furiously, with my fists. I pounded the wall again and again, until my fists were red with blood. "Granddad, Granddad," I screamed, as tears rolled down my checks, but there was no answer. I was at a standstill. I felt helpless and defeated.

All of a sudden I noticed a bright light glowing at the base of the wall. It was the large golden book.

"They must have left it behind," I said to myself.

Picking it up, I was amazed to find that though it was very big, it also was extremely light. When I opened the book, the brilliance of the pages temporarily blinded me. They were not made of paper, but of light. And the letters on the pages were written in flames of red and gold. I shivered as I read the words:

You're missing it!

Heaven is all around you!

And you're missing it!

That empty,
        hollow feeling—
    that desperate, lonely feeling
  that disturbs you
    will continue to haunt you,
        as long as you continue to see life
            from your present perspective.

There is a path
  through the emptiness…
    a path through the loneliness…
      a path to the truth.

Within you is a guide,
  a quiet, gentle guide,
    who knows your every need
    and your every longing.

Listen within
  for that
    still,
      small
        voice –
          that quiet, gentle voice,
          that voice that is me,
          that voice that is you,
            and it will show you
                the way.

As you become ready,
        more dreams will follow.

        Each will guide you,
            if you let it.

        Each will lead you
            through the emptiness.

                    But first,
                you must decide
            if you're up for the journey,
                for it could be
                a perilous one.

If you make it,…

        You will have found the answers
    to many of your questions…

            The answers that you and so
        many others have sought
                since the beginning of time!

\

2 Flashes of Insight

I heard a soft whisper, "Uncle David, Uncle David, wake up. Mama told me to come wake you up."

My eyes opened to Alex's smiling face.

He stood by my bed until I sat up. He had his dump truck in his right hand. It was interesting to me that the dump truck was his favorite. Dump trucks had always been one of my favorite toys, too.

"You run along," I said. "I'll be in there in a minute."

"Okay," he replied, dashing from the room.

Suddenly, the words from the dream book flashed back into my mind, tongues of fire leaping from each letter. I could see the words, as if the book were right in front of me. "What a dream," I said aloud. "It was so lifelike… And the words in the book… I need to find a pen. I need to write them down!"

Usually I forgot dreams as soon as I awoke. Not this time. The words from the book were branded in my mind. Tongues of fire continued to leap from the letters in my head as I fashioned them on the page. My hands trembled as I hurried to write them all down. Then I realized there was no need to hurry since the words dominated my thoughts. They weren't going anywhere until they had been written.

As I wrote the final letter, a feeling of great peace came over me. The words in my mind lost their flames, now becoming soft and comforting.

I read the words over and over again, somewhat in awe. I had had many dreams in my life, but none like this one, and I wasn't really sure what to do with it. Had God just spoken to me or was my subconscious playing tricks at my expense? I thought about finding Jenny and telling her about my dream to see what she thought, but I decided against it. Instead, I opted to wait and see if there really were more dreams to follow before I told anyone about the crazy, yet miraculous dream I had just experienced.

As I ate breakfast that morning, the dream stayed with me. Images of the wall, the stream, Granddad and his companions flowed through my thoughts. The words from the dream book played and replayed themselves in my mind. The possibility of finally finding the answers to some of my questions was intriguing to me. I hoped that more dreams would come, and that they would come soon.

After breakfast, Jenny and Alex headed out, Jenny to work and Alex to day-care, while I headed to the bathroom for a long, hot bath. Baths always relaxed me. They were one of those simple pleasures that seemed to calm my ever-present anxiety.

That morning, while I lay in the tub, I continued to think about the dream and the decision it called for. Really there was no decision. There was no way I would ever turn down the opportunity to learn the truth about life, no matter how much danger I had to face.

After a lengthy bath, I drove over to Granddad's. As I pulled into his driveway, I was shocked by the barrenness of his yard. It didn't look anything like the yard he had had in North Carolina, which was always full of flowers. This yard was empty except for the dogwood by the road and the half dead holly bush at the corner of the house.

The house itself, however, looked much better than the yard. It was white with a forest green door and shutters to match. There was an inviting front porch with a swing at one end and a couple of bentwood rockers at the other. It was a nice house, and I could see why Granddad had chosen to live there, in spite of the yard. Besides, I was sure it wouldn't be long before Granddad would have this yard looking as lush as his yard in North Carolina.

No one came when I knocked at the front door, so I wandered around back to see if Granddad was there. Sure enough, that's where I found him, sitting beneath a large mimosa tree with his legs crossed and his eyes closed. He was a perfect picture of peace and harmony. Seeing him there reminded me of when I was young. Jenny and I used to laugh at Granddad when we saw him meditating. When he heard us, he would laugh, too. He even tried to show us how to meditate a few times, but we couldn't sit still long enough, and we would inevitably lose interest.

I didn't learn how to meditate until my last year in seminary. It helped slow me down, reducing some of that ceaseless chatter in my mind. After learning how, I regretted not listening to Granddad's instructions when I was younger. Listening to him back then could have saved me a lot of needless frustration.

Rather than disturb him, I found a place to sit on the steps leading up to the back porch. Sitting there, I saw that the backyard needed at least as much work as the front, but it was a level lot and it, too, had potential. I could see into the garage. It was full of junk, as Granddad had said, and it definitely needed emptying.

After a minute or so, Granddad opened his eyes. "Good morning," he said, and then he slowly stood up.

"Yes, it's a beautiful morning, and how are you?" I asked in reply.

"Couldn't be better."

I believed him; it was written all over his face.

"How often do you meditate, Granddad?"

"Usually a couple of times a day," he said, as he walked my way.

"For how long?"

"I don't know, probably twenty minutes to an hour each time. It just depends on what's happening that day."

"How do you find time to do it that often and for that long?"

"I make time. Everyone makes time for what's really important to him. My life feels better when I'm centered, and going into the silence centers me, so I make time for it. Which reminds me of a story. You wanna hear it?"

"Sure."

"It's about the monk, Martin Luther, who lived back in the 1500's. You probably studied him when you were in seminary, didn't you?"

I nodded and Granddad began his story:

> Martin Luther was no ordinary monk. He was extremely dedicated to his spiritual life. In fact, he usually spent about two hours in prayer and meditation every morning before he began his day.
>
> One day, the day before a very important religious holiday, one of the younger monks approached Martin Luther, saying, "Sir, are you planning to do your usual amount of prayer this morning?"
>
> "No, I'm not," he replied.
>
> "Good," said the young monk, quite relieved, "because we have a lot of work to do today and I fear that we might not get it all done by the beginning of the festival tomorrow."
>
> Martin Luther replied, "You're right, we do have a lot to do. I've been concerned myself. No, today, instead of praying two hours, I'm going to pray three, for I know that if I don't, we'll never get all of this work done."

I grinned at the story's ending and said, "I bet that younger monk was surprised by Martin Luther's reply."

"I bet he was, too," said Granddad. "Most people don't feel they have time to go into the silence everyday. I, on the other hand, look at it much like Martin Luther; I can't afford not to meditate everyday. And on more strenuous days, I, too, tend to spend more time in the silence, rather than less."

I pondered his words in light of my own situation. I had meditated very little since starting my job search. I'd been too busy.

He continued, "But you know, if you can't seem to find time to meditate, you may need to try a different approach to getting yourself slowed down and centered. Some people run, others go for long walks, and some take long hot baths. There are many things you can do that will help you gather yourself. Meditation has proven to be one of the best methods, but it's not always the best for everybody, at least not at first."

Then he said, "Well, you about ready to get started?" and he began to walk toward the garage.

I didn't reply; I was still reflecting. Then I said, "I guess so. It doesn't seem to be emptying by itself, does it?… It looks like a big job."

Evidently, the people who had rented the house before Granddad were not the tidiest people in the world. It was a jumbled mess.

"How do you want to handle this?" I asked, not really sure where to begin.

"We're aiming to move it all to the street to be picked up, so just grab something and let's go," he replied.

We spent much of the next few hours walking back and forth from the garage to the road. We carried all kinds of things: old lamps, a broken down bicycle with split tires, two rusted out fenders, a broken weight bench, an old basketball rim, and many other useless items.

As we walked back and forth, I noticed that Granddad seemed to be enjoying every second as he worked. He silently carried things to the street, a slight smile ever-present on his face, and then he casually strolled back for more. He seemed so light on his feet, as if his feet never quite touched the ground. He looked much as he had when he was meditating. I was amazed at how he kept going without showing any sign of fatigue. And though I was in pretty good shape and much younger, the work was beginning to get to me.

"Hey Granddad, let's take a break and talk awhile."

"Would you like some water or some orange juice?" he asked in reply.

"Orange juice would be great."

I sat down on the back steps while Granddad got a pitcher of juice and glasses. I guzzled the first glass and then poured another. Granddad slowly sipped his, seeming to relish each drop. I drank three glasses before he was halfway through his first.

It was apparent that Granddad and I lived in two totally different worlds. His was a slow, peaceful world in which everything was enjoyed, even work. Mine was a frantic, "let's get it all done as soon as we can, so we can do something else" kind of world.

"Granddad, there is something different about you."

"What do you mean?"

"I'm not sure. It's like you're the same person that you used to be, yet in a way you're different. It's like you are more you than you used to be, if that makes any sense. I mean, you have always seemed pretty happy, but now you've turned it up a notch or two." I paused for a moment to think. His eyes gazed into mine as he waited for me to continue. "You seem so content. That's what it is; you seem totally content."

We sat quietly. I reflected on my realization about Granddad and the sight of him slowly, peacefully carrying junk to the road. My whole life had been one of hurrying from one thing to the next, hardly enjoying one accomplishment, before feeling the need to head off in a different direction to reach another goal.

"Granddad, what did you do during those years you were gone to create such a change?"

"David, I'm not sure what you're talking about. I didn't really do anything different, other than spend a lot more time in the silence. I do feel content, but that's not anything new."

"There's something different," I insisted. Whatever his secret was, I wanted to know it. "Well, whether you are different or not," I continued, "how did you find such peace and contentment?"

"I'm not sure this is the answer you're looking for, but I didn't find contentment until I quit searching for it," he said with a shrug of his shoulders.

"Come on, Granddad," I said. "Tell me." I wasn't going to let him off that easily.

"David, I'm not trying to avoid your question, but it's been a long process. It took me forty years to get where I am. I spent the first thirty or so searching and then the next few learning how to accept, let go and stop searching. For years, much of my free time was spent digesting self-help books and workshops. Though the books helped at first, they weren't able to assist me as much as I had hoped.

"Then one day, the truth of my situation hit me. No writer or speaker that I'd ever met had ever reached enlightenment. Why was I looking to them for answers? I had to find my own path. My gut said that spending more time alone and meditating everyday was the place to start. I didn't really have any idea what an impact meditation would have, but it seemed like the thing to do. Once I quit looking elsewhere for the answers and listened within…" He left the sentence unfinished.

He paused and sipped his juice. He held up the glass so that light shone through. "Liquid sunshine. A beautiful color."

He turned his head toward me and said, "Am I talking too much?"

"Oh no," I answered without hesitation.

He smiled and said, "When you feel it's overload, tell me."

I promised I would.

He went on slowly, "I struggled with meditation for over a year. Doubts about how much it was helping got in the way. My mind would reach a state of peace during meditation, but later, it would regress to a state of chaos. Finally, I took a meditation class, and that helped my technique, as well as my confidence. Gradually, I began to see results. The constant chatter in my mind became more manageable, and the voice of my true, natural self sounded louder and clearer.

I realized I was listening closely… more attentively than I had for some time. And I thought I knew why. My grandfather was not telling me where I was wrong, not telling me what to do.

I had heard so many fire and brimstone sermons that told the congregation how sinful they were, as though the ministers were capable of judging everyone. Those sermons had always turned me off.

Granddad, on the other hand, was relating the path he had found for himself. I liked his approach. It would be up to me to try it or not.

Granddad continued, "I found myself going through an emptying process, and my view of the world became different. Few things were cut and dry, and many of my long-held beliefs no longer seemed true."

The more Granddad spoke, the closer I listened. He had always just been Granddad to me, and now all of a sudden, I was seeing him in a new light.

"Over the years," Granddad said, "we accumulate a lot of stuff in our heads: thoughts about ourselves and others, and thoughts about how life works. The things that we learned when we were young don't always work for us as we age. But rather than changing our ways to fit adult reality, we try to make reality fit our beliefs.

"Our minds are filled with so much junk that there is little room for anything new."

"Yeah, kinda like this garage," I replied.

"Exactly," he said. "We are cleaning out this garage so that it can be more useful. We must also empty our minds of some of our old dysfunctional beliefs, so that there is room for some new, healthier ones.

"What we want, admit it or not, is to grow without having to let go of our old ways. We want things to be better and to stay the same all at once… which is impossible, of course.

"That's where meditation comes in. It teaches us to let go. That's a tall order for most people, especially Americans. Here in the U.S., we have been taught to seek the *American Dream.* We've been told that if we work hard, we can have whatever we want. We can have it all; everything is ours for the taking. So most people bust their butts trying to get all they can, all the while discontent with what they have. They miss life as they struggle to achieve *The Dream.* They try to buy their way into Heaven on Earth. But Heaven on Earth can't be purchased. It can be experienced, but not purchased. There's nothing wrong with having things, but they'll never get you to heaven."

When Granddad mentioned heaven, my mind flashed back to the words in the dream book. It, too, had spoken of heaven, saying, *"You're missing it! Heaven is all around you! And you're missing it!"* I considered telling Granddad about my dream, but again I decided to wait and see if more dreams really were coming.

Granddad finished by saying, "Peace and contentment come to us when we let go of the search and follow our inner guidance. Heaven is where God is, and God is everywhere. All we have to do is trust the process of our lives and open ourselves to the truth and heaven is ours. It's as simple as that, and we don't have to wait until we die."

There was truth in what Granddad said; I could feel it. But he made it sound so easy, and it didn't feel that easy to me. First of all, I wasn't convinced that searching wouldn't help. Besides, I wasn't sure I could quit searching, anyway. I'd spent my whole life doing it.

Secondly, I wasn't into material things, but I did like money. I had been a saver since childhood, and I had always figured that a million dollars would help me feel more at peace. A million dollars would free me from having to work, and it would enable me to satisfy the few material needs I did have, but most importantly, it would help me feel secure.

But what if he was right? What if heaven could be experienced right now, and I didn't have to have a lot of money or material possessions to experience it?

"You about ready to get back to this garage?" Granddad said, bringing me back from my reverie. He had given me a lot to think about. I wanted to be content like Granddad, but I wasn't convinced that it was possible.

"Yeah, let's finish it up," I replied.

Back in the garage, I picked up a torn lamp shade. Underneath it was a small toy dump truck. As I picked it up and looked it over, Granddad's words about emptying came back to mind. Emptying was one of the main functions of a dump truck. It seemed ironic that it showed up right after our talk. I decided to tuck it away in my pocket for Alex.

We finished cleaning the garage before noon. I headed home to Jenny's, ate some lunch, and took a nap. After waking, I took my guitar out on the porch and played it until Jenny and Alex came home.

Alex was fascinated with my guitar. He wanted to pluck the strings himself. So after I played a few songs for him and Jenny, I let Alex play some, too.

"Look at me, Mom," he said proudly, as all kinds of noise came from the guitar.

"If you keep at it, you could be a real guitar player one day," she replied. "You might even learn to play as well as Uncle David."

While I was playing, Jenny asked if I would be willing to play a few songs at a birthday party for one of her friends. The party would be a week from Friday. I hated the pressure that came with entertaining, but something inside told me to say, "yes," so I agreed. Doing well in whatever I did had always been important to me, and the possibility of screwing up and embarrassing myself hung like an ax over my head each moment of a performance. I would have to do a lot of practicing in the next few days to feel comfortable playing in front of people again.

That night, I went to bed with my mind racing. My talks with Granddad, my upcoming musical performance, and all the things I wanted to accomplish before beginning my new job, filled my head. I had to find a place to live. I also had hoped to buy a new car. My old Duster was on its last leg. It had gotten me through high school, college, and seminary, but it was time for it to retire.

The next morning, I awoke feeling anxious and overwhelmed. School would start soon. There was so little time. Whenever stress raised its ugly head, my pattern was to get busier, to push harder. And more often than not things just became worse. I decided to start looking for a new car.

My first day of car shopping was less than wonderful. I was in a hurry to finish, so I could get started on the rest of my tasks. The salesman who greeted me at the first lot was a short, thin, middle-aged man with greasy hair. He was on me before I was even out of my car, obviously hungry for a sale. At the next two lots, the salesmen looked less slimy, but they were just as pushy as the first. It quickly became apparent that buying a new car was not going to be an easy, enjoyable experience. The salesmen knew their roles much better than I knew mine. I felt as though I were swimming among a school of sharks circling for the kill. Being ripped off seemed inevitable.

The next day was more of the same. After visiting three lots, I headed home low on energy and feeling somewhat dejected. None of the salesmen seemed at all trustworthy, and none of the cars so far was close to what I wanted. There were only two lots left in the immediate area that sold any of the types of cars I might want to buy. I decided to go by Granddad's and discuss the situation with him.

He said, "Don't think and figure so much, just trust your gut."

"But this is a lot of money that I'll be spending," I replied. "I don't want to make a bad deal or end up with a lemon."

"It *is* quite a bit of money," he replied, "but your inner self knows what you need, and it also knows what you need to learn. It will do you right."

Trusting my gut was not going to be easy, especially when it came to spending thousands of dollars. I left Granddad's still feeling confused and frustrated, and went to bed that night feeling the same.

The next morning, I awoke with an image of a light blue automobile in my head. There had not been such a car on any of the lots I had visited. As I wiped the sleep from my eyes, parts of a dream began to come back to me. I was on a car lot, standing beside a light blue car. In fact, it was the only car on the lot. The rest were dump trucks of different sizes and colors, some as small as Alex's truck, others as large as houses. All of a sudden, one of the bigger ones, a large golden dump truck, began to move. It turned toward me and began to roll in my direction. I turned to run from it. It slowly rolled after me. Then I heard its whistle blow behind me. The sound spurred me to run even faster. After running for what seemed like forever, I glanced back over my shoulder to see the truck coming to a halt. It was a good thing, because my energy was depleted; I couldn't have run much farther.

The door of the truck opened, and out jumped Granddad. We walked toward each other. He had the golden book from my first dream under his arm.

"It's a lot easier if you don't resist so much," he said.

"Resist what?" I asked.

"The dump truck, silly," he replied. Then he turned and began to walk back toward the truck with the book still under his arm.

I was surprised and disappointed, thinking that he was going to give me the book to read, and instead he was keeping it. "Granddad, aren't you going to let me see the book?"

"Oh, so you do want to learn, just not from the dump truck," he said. "You need to realize that some teaching comes free, whether you want it or not, but there is another kind, which only comes upon request." Then he handed me the book.

I opened it, and again the light from the pages blinded me for a few moments until my eyes adjusted to their brightness. Again the words burned like red and gold flames as they danced upon the pages of glowing white light.

*You can run from
and avoid the emptiness
for only so long;
it will keep coming back!*

Remember,
the only way past the emptiness
is through it.

To go through it,
you must first
open your awareness.

It's not as scary as it seems –
not as hard as it looks.

So,
step back
from the drama
that is your life.

Step back
and observe
your feelings and thoughts.

Step back
and take note of
all the many things
happening around you.

Become
   aware
      of the positives and negatives
         within you.

But do not embrace them.

They aren't you!

You are
   that which
      observes and experiences.

Don't flee
   from the emptiness.

   Instead,
stroll into it, as you might
   stroll into a gentle spring shower.

   Your spirits may be dampened initially,
     but the dampness will pass,
       and then
     you will step into
      an experience
     beyond your imagination.

     You will step into the light
       and the truth of reality itself.

Another dream *had* come, just as the first one had said it would, and though it was weird like the first dream, it seemed a little easier to understand. At least, it was easier to make sense of why certain things were in the dream. Dump trucks had shown up a lot in my life over the last few days, so it seemed logical that dump trucks might appear in my dream. Cars had been my focus of late, so having a car in my dream seemed to fit, as well. But I couldn't figure out why Granddad made me ask for the dream book. It appeared that he had intended to give it to me, or else he wouldn't have brought it with him.

I pondered the dream and its meaning while eating breakfast and while getting dressed for another day of car shopping.

When I reached the first car lot that morning, a light blue Camry was displayed in the very front of the lot. Incredible! It was the car I had seen in my dream. It was beautiful and it was equipped with everything I wanted, including mud flaps, cruise control, and power door locks. I dickered with the salesman some, and an hour later, it was mine.

It's funny how riding in your own, brand new car can make you feel so good and bring such an enormous smile to your face. I probably looked pretty silly riding home grinning from ear to ear, but hiding my feelings had never been a strong suit of mine. When I felt like a king, it was easy to see, and when I was depressed or sad, it was just as obvious.

At home, I showed off my new wheels to Jenny and Alex. Jenny was impressed, but Alex said he would have chosen a jeep or a dump truck. After taking them for a ride, I headed to Granddad's to show him my car and to tell him about my two dreams.

Granddad was sitting on the steps of his front porch when I drove up.

"So you did get the blue one instead of a dump truck," he called to me, as he walked down the steps.

My mouth dropped wide open. "What do you mean, 'the blue one instead of a dump truck?'" I asked.

"Well, you trusted your dream guide, didn't you? It wasn't so hard after all, was it?"

My head was spinning. "How do you know about my dream?"

"I just open my mind, and all kinds of revelations come in. You ought to try it," he replied, as he walked toward the backyard.

"Hold on a second, Granddad. You're going too fast for me," I said, running to catch up with him.

"I'll walk slower then," he answered with a grin.

"I wasn't talking about how fast you were walking. You know what I meant. How did you know about my dream?"

"I told you," he said, and then he continued around the corner of the house, leaving me standing there, dumbfounded. My thoughts were shooting in all directions. I felt my world had just lost some of its foundation, some of its fundamental rules. I'd been told that some people could read minds, but I'd never met anyone who could really do it.

I don't know how long I stood there dazed and confused, my mind trying to sort through Granddad's words. It seemed like an eternity, but suddenly, my mind settled, and I had a flash of insight. When I added together my first dream, my talks with Granddad, his moving to Birmingham, and my second dream, everything made perfect sense. Granddad had come to Birmingham to be my teacher, but I had to ask him to do it. I went straight to find him.

"I will," he said, before my request even left my lips. "I'm glad to see you're finally opening to some of the revelations around you."

This mind reading stuff was going to take some getting used to, I thought to myself.

"It's not that hard," he said in reply, as if I had said the words aloud. "It's just a matter of openness and selection of sensory input."

Shaking my head from side to side and sitting down on the ground, I pinched my arm to make sure I wasn't dreaming.

"So you know about my first dream, too?"

He nodded in reply.

"Well, what now?" I asked, not really knowing what else to say.

"What do you mean?"

"When do we start the lessons?"

"They've started. Can't you tell?" Then he paused before saying, "But David, you need to realize that I won't be your only instructor. In fact, you will have lots of teachers. I'm just one of many. I won't even be your primary instructor."

"Then who will?"

"Your inner guide, of course. It's the only teacher you really need. I'm just here because your inner guide and my inner guide brought us together. You don't really need me, but my being here may speed up your progress a bit.

"And then of course, the universe will be one of your main instructors. Your inner guide leads you, and the universe creates the dramas from which you can learn and balance yourself. The universe is very much into balance. And it has some *BIG* plans for you, so you'd better get ready."

"Granddad, slow down. You're talking in riddles."

"Okay, let's start over," he said. "There are millions of teachers in this world, but really in a sense, there are only two: your gut and the universe."

"What about God?" I asked.

"If you bring God into the picture, then there's really only one teacher, because God's a part of everything that is: you, me, the universe, etc. But usually, I don't talk about God much, or at least I don't use the word, 'God,' because the word doesn't mean the same thing to everybody. For some, God's a giant old man with a long beard who lives in the sky. For others, God's the great judge of mankind. Still others see God as love. And then there are those who say they don't believe in God per se; instead, they believe in a higher power, the Oneness, or nature. I'm not sure that *anyone* really knows what God is, and since the word creates so much confusion and division at times, I just don't use it very often.

"Anyway... you, like everyone else in the world, are on a journey toward wholeness. The guide for your journey is your gut. Everything that happens to you occurs to help you find yourself and to help you realize your oneness with the universe. Is that better?"

"Yeah, a little, I guess."

"And the best part about it is that you don't have to do any-thing but open yourself to the process, and the truth will come to you."

"It can't be that easy," I replied. "I've spent most of my life looking for the truth, and I haven't found it yet."

"I'm not saying it's easy. What I'm saying is that searching often prevents finding. Openness is the way. Now, what I want you to do is to go into the house and get the pencil and note-book from my dining room table."

I took a few brisk steps toward the house before Granddad said, "Slow down."

"But I want to hurry and get started. This is exciting!" I replied.

"We've got plenty of time," he said, "but if you want to get started right away, you'd do better by beginning to practice patience and awareness, rather than continuing your old habit of hurrying. Walk slowly and be aware of your body. Notice how you feel and how your body moves as you go."

I could sense the possibilities before me, and it was all I could do to slowly walk up the steps and not take off at a trot. The pencil and notebook were just where he had said they would be. I eagerly picked them up, curious as to what Granddad was going to do next and started to hurry back. I caught myself, slowing to a walk. It felt strange to slow down and consciously pay attention to my movements. I had not been aware of being so out of touch with my body. It was clearly a surprise to me and it felt disconcerting.

When I handed Granddad the notebook and pencil, he said, "Now, find yourself a comfortable place to sit and meditate for a while. Then I have a few questions for you to ponder."

"What are they?"

"*After* you meditate. Let's do one thing at a time," he said with a chuckle. "Be patient. It's a good habit to slow yourself down and get centered before starting any endeavor."

I followed his directions. I grabbed a lawn chair and placed it in a shady spot under the mimosa tree. Granddad surprised me by pulling up a chair and sitting directly across from me.

"Would you like to learn a new way of meditating?" he asked.

"Sure," I said excitedly.

"Okay. Close your eyes, and get yourself into a relaxed position." Granddad's voice became slower and deeper, "Now, become aware of your body... Notice if there is any tension anywhere in your body... Don't try to get rid of it, or resist it... Just become aware of it... Now, become aware of your breathing."

He proceeded to take me through a process of tensing and relaxing virtually every part of my body. Every so often along the way, he would get me to repeat some things silently to myself. He would have me say things like, "My shoulders are relaxed. My body is relaxed. I am content and at ease." The phrases sounded foreign to me at first. I felt silly repeating them, but my body did start to relax. And as my body began to let go, so did my mind, and all of the chatter in my brain ceased. I had never experienced such depths of relaxation.

Then Granddad moved me into a meditation technique which helped me become more aware of my breathing. My mind became empty and peaceful, and strangely enough, I felt connected to everything around me. It was an extraordinary feeling.

Granddad finished the meditation by having me get in touch with the many drives and feelings within me, and he encouraged me to accept them all. During this latter part of the process, I also became more aware of the difference between the voice of my inner self and all of the other feelings and voices within me. The whole experience was unlike any other in my life.

When it came time to bring me back from my meditative state, he did it very slowly, having me open my eyes a little at a time. Then he had me sit for a while with my eyes open, yet still focusing on my breath and the things around me. Feelings of great love and appreciation began to overwhelm me, and tears came to my eyes. I felt totally open and free – no thoughts, no expectations, no judgments, and no anxiety. I was totally relaxed.

"Notice how you feel when you finish a deep meditation," he said in a low, soft voice. "That is a taste of heaven and the feeling of connection that comes with it. See how empty and free your mind is. The chatter is gone. We can live this way almost all of the time, free of the endless wants, worries, and obsessions that drive us.

"While you are in this free state, I want you to open your awareness to who you are – your gifts, what you enjoy and what you want most from life. I want you to find your purpose. Remember the target I drew for you the other day? You need to figure out what fits in the bull's-eye of your target. Narrow it down to three or four things. And take your time. There's no hurry." Granddad lived his own words, speaking slowly. The words were unhurried and his tone soothing.

"Finding out who you are is the most important thing you can do. When we don't understand ourselves, we stumble through life, latching on to one addiction or another, trying to avoid the pain and emptiness of life, often hurting others as we go. Not knowing what we are about skews our sense of boundaries. Anxiety, overeating, alcoholism, co-dependence, or some other addiction is inevitably the result.

"When you know who you are, you intuitively know your path and your place in the universe as well. And you have no need to fight the emptiness. You begin to feel full just because you're alive. You have a good sense of boundaries, and addictions lose their power over you. Then, and only then, can you really impact the world and the people in it in a truly loving and compassionate way.

"Many of the world's problems would disappear if everyone could just get a grip on who they are. So listen inside and see what comes up.

"I'll be around. Come find me when you've finished. If nothing comes to you today, don't worry about it. It'll come, eventually. Remember, don't push, just be easy and patient with yourself. Open to what comes."

There was no doubt in my mind what belonged in the bull's-eye of my target. I knew what I wanted. I wanted to understand the mysteries of life and to be content like Granddad was. I also wanted a good, loving relationship and financial security.

Figuring out who I was did not come as easily, however. At first, the only answers that came to me were relational answers. I was a brother, a teacher, a friend, and a grandson. Then my thoughts shifted to traits about myself such as being caring, anxious, and restless.

It wasn't until I started exploring my place in the universe that I began to get an idea of who I really was. I saw myself as a child of God. I was both a mortal human being and an eternal, spiritual being. But surely Granddad was looking for more than that. Those truths seemed pretty self-evident and mundane. I wanted to give Granddad a more impressive answer.

After wrestling with myself for over an hour, I finally wrote down, "I am an infinite spiritual being in a finite world. I'm doing the best I can to make it, like everyone else. I guess I am in the process of realizing who I truly am, and it's not an easy job."

It wasn't really a very impressive answer, but it was the best I could come up with.

I went to find Granddad to show him my answer. He was sitting on the front steps petting a small tabby. I sat down beside him, handing him what I'd written.

"This is Tinker; she lives next door," said Granddad, introducing me to the cat. Tinker proceeded to walk over and put her head under my hand so that I would pet her. "Tinker's a master at the art of living in the moment," Granddad continued. "She doesn't worry about the future. If you watch her closely, you can learn a lot from her."

I rubbed Tinker's head while Granddad glanced over my written thoughts. After a few moments of petting, Tinker started to purr. Then she jumped up into my lap.

"This is good," Granddad said, after he had finished reading my answer.

"So, I'm right," I replied.

"That's not what I said. I said, 'This is good.' It's not a matter of right or wrong."

"What do you mean?"

"Truth comes to us on a continuum. There are some answers which are closer to the truth than yours and some that are further away."

"But I thought truth was absolute, that there's only one truth."

"And you're right," Granddad replied, "but because we're imperfect beings, or rather we haven't realized our perfection yet, we usually only receive part of the truth at a time."

"Well then, any answer would have been okay."

"Yeah, pretty much so. It's not a competition. It's just a starting point. It gives you a place from which to begin, and it gives me an indication of how much truth you've realized up to this point in your life. As you open to the truth, you'll acquire a new, more accurate sense of reality, and then your answers will change."

"But how do you know for sure if your answers are true and based in reality, or just illusions?" I asked.

"I only know of one sure way to tell. Down through the ages, it has been said, 'The best way to judge a tree is by its fruits.' Healthy trees bear healthy fruit. It's the same with beliefs. If a belief produces health, peace, love, and contentment over time, then it has truth, so keep it. At least, keep it until you find something better. If a belief creates extreme guilt, ill health, pain, or misery, then reexamine it. You might need to trade it in for a new and healthier one... And speaking of new... When are you going to take me for a ride in this new, dream car of yours?"

"Right now, if you're ready," I said, placing Tinker on the step beside me.

"Let's do it," said Granddad.

And off we went.

3 A New Reality

It was close to a week before I saw Granddad again. Though I was excited about learning from him, my desire to find an apartment before school started took priority, so I spent the next few days looking through newspapers, making phone calls, and looking at apartments. When I wasn't looking for an apartment, I was practicing my guitar for Jenny's upcoming party. Once again, I found myself pushing to get things done.

After four days of fruitless apartment hunting, it appeared that I would be staying with Jenny longer than I had planned. I had seen fifteen apartments, and none was suitable. Five were too expensive, six were in unsafe neighborhoods, two smelled of mildew, and two others were just not what I wanted. In fact, none of the ones I had seen was even remotely close to what I was looking for. Then on Wednesday, with only four days left until school was to begin, in the midst of giving up hope, I saw an ad in the paper for an apartment that was just two blocks from Jenny's house.

The apartment was on the top floor of an old mansion that had been converted into six, two-bedroom apartments. It had high ceilings, large rooms, a balcony, a fireplace, and even a walk-in closet. It was perfect, almost too good to be true. Experience had taught me that when something seemed too good to be true, it usually was, so I had reservations. There was always a catch somewhere. The price wasn't too bad, though it was more than I had intended to pay. Still, my gut said to take it in spite of my doubts and the extra expense, so I did.

Nothing unusual or extraordinary happened during my apartment hunting experience. But right after I signed the lease, one of the other tenants told me of an interesting tale concerning the building's previous owner. Supposedly, the owner had been a wealthy, senile man, and it was rumored that when he died he left hidden jewels somewhere in the building.

The possibility of instant wealth was intriguing to me, so as soon as I moved in, I began exploring. After thirty minutes of searching cabinets and closets, I decided that if there were any diamonds and rubies in that big old house, they were definitely in one of the other apartments.

Once I had my place in order, my thoughts shifted gears to the upcoming party. I had only a day and a half left to practice, and I could feel my anxiety rising. Even though I had played at quite a few parties and in front of large groups numerous times in college and seminary, I still hadn't learned how to relax before or during a performance. My need for perfection and fear of negative judgment always got in the way.

Friday evening as I entered the apartment complex where the party was to be held my shoulders were tight and butterflies filled my stomach. After winding through the complex, I came to the pool and clubhouse area where I'd be playing.

There were only a few guests present when I arrived, but more wandered in while I was setting up. I was surprised to find that most of the guests seemed to be women without dates. I had been so focused on my performance that the thought of meeting people had not even crossed my mind.

When most of the guests had arrived, I decided to go ahead and begin my mini concert. I led off with a couple of songs by the Eagles and followed with a few by James Taylor. After I had everyone warmed up, including myself, I decided to play a few of my more showy tunes: "Piano Man" by Billy Joel, and "Heart of Gold" by Neil Young, both with harmonica parts. Putting on my harmonica holder and playing the guitar and harmonica simultaneously brought a big round of applause, and suddenly I was the center of attention. Next came my funny songs, "Dear Abby" and "Oh Lord, It's Hard to Be

Humble," and a few lesser known tunes. "Oh Lord, It's Hard to Be Humble" was kind of an absurd song for me to sing, since I was naturally both humble and shy when singing in front of anyone, but especially in front of a large group.

As the evening wore on, I found myself singing to one particular woman. She had shoulder length blond hair and the prettiest blue eyes I'd ever seen. She was wearing a pink and blue pastel top with white shorts, which showed off her petite figure. The longer I played, the more I found myself looking her way, and every time I looked, she was looking at me, too. The attraction was unusually strong; I could feel it in my gut, as well as in the rest of my body. It wasn't a sexual feeling. It was different. During a break, I asked about her, and Jenny said that her name was Lynn.

Even though there had been a lot of eye contact between the two of us while I was singing and there seemed to be a mutual attraction, I felt reluctant to go up and introduce myself. Jenny offered to introduce us, but I declined. I told her that maybe I would take her up on her offer after I'd finished playing, but I knew that I probably wouldn't.

After an hour and a half of picking and singing, I finally called it quits, finishing with a couple of songs by Kenny Loggins. When I was through, everyone gave me a standing ovation, which made me feel good but also embarrassed. I could feel my face flushing. I had never been the kind to play it cool and act as though applause were no big deal. Shyly, I stepped back to the microphone and said, "Thanks." Then I bent to put my guitar in its case. Looking at me, a stranger might have guessed that something terrible had just happened, instead of the fact that I had just given one of the best performances of my life. The applause filled me with all kinds of mixed feelings; I loved it and hated it all at once.

As I was closing the lid on my guitar case, a woman's voice said, "You're very good."

I turned to look up into Lynn's beautiful eyes, shocked to find her standing behind me.

"Where did you get those funny songs?" she asked. "I've

never heard some of them before. Did you write them?"

"No, I just play 'em, but they're my favorites," I replied and then went silent, not knowing what else to say to this woman.

"May I see that?" she asked, pointing to my harmonica holder. "How do you put it on?"

I helped her put the odd-looking metal contraption over her head.

"Where's your harmonica?" she asked.

I opened my guitar case, retrieved a harmonica, and snapped it into the holder. As I did this, an eerie feeling came over me. I had the distinct feeling that I was being watched and that danger was near. I turned to see if anybody was looking our way, but I didn't see anyone paying us any attention. I tried to dismiss the feeling, but it wouldn't completely go away.

Lynn began to blow on the harmonica. After blowing it a few times, she laughed and said, "This is neat. How'd you learn to play the harmonica and the guitar at the same time? Isn't that difficult to do?"

"It's a lot easier than it looks."

She blew on the harmonica a few more times and then stopped and said, "I didn't introduce myself. I'm Lynn Whitmire."

"And I'm David Harper," I replied.

"Yeah, I know. Jenny told me that you're her brother and that you just moved to town."

"Yeah, about two weeks ago. I moved here to start a new job."

"Where?"

"At Fair Hope Treatment Center. I'll be teaching school to troubled teenagers."

"That's similar to what I do. I'm a social worker at a drug and alcohol treatment center."

"I bet that's tough work."

"Sometimes, but usually I enjoy it." She paused before continuing, "Jenny said you just finished seminary. Aren't you going to be a minister?"

"No, at least not in a church," I replied.

"But isn't that why someone goes to seminary?" she questioned with a perplexed look on her face.

"Some do," I said. "But others become counselors or chaplains in hospitals. I just want to teach. I went to seminary to learn. You know, to figure life out for myself."

"Did you get it all figured out?" she asked playfully.

"I wish," I replied with a smile.

I couldn't believe my luck. I couldn't believe Lynn had come right up to me and introduced herself.

Lynn and I talked the rest of the evening. By the time the party was over, we had grown amazingly close for two people who had just met. Unfortunately, the eerie feeling of being watched stayed with me. I caught myself periodically glancing around to see if I could catch someone looking our way. I was sure someone was watching me. Still, it was a good evening, and as we said, "Good night," Lynn surprised me by inviting me to meet her for church on Sunday. Even though I was not much of a church goer, I jumped at the offer.

That night, I lay awake thinking about Lynn and how assertive she had been. Even though I could make friends easily, meeting women had always been a challenge for me. I also thought about Granddad and about school beginning on Monday. With all of the excitement, sleep arrived slowly.

Finally asleep, my unconscious took over. It was a restless slumber with much dreaming. I found myself at a party sitting on a sofa talking with a beautiful woman. She had blond hair and blue eyes, and she looked a lot like Lynn. My attention was not on the woman, however. It was focused on a pair of eyes staring out at me from the darkness surrounding the party. I watched anxiously as the eyes began to move steadily toward me. It wasn't long before a large, dark-haired man with deep-set eyes stepped from the emptiness into the light. I began to tremble. I felt the need to do something, but I didn't know what. I didn't recognize the man, but I sensed a great hatred for me within him.

Then the man disappeared and the dark emptiness

surrounding the party filled with light. Granddad stepped out from the center of the light holding the bright shining, golden book. He gave it to me, and I opened it to read:

All of your effort
to fix and control the world
and everyone in it
only enhances your feelings of
emptiness and lack.

Wake up!

Heaven is
the experience of oneness
which comes with
the willingness
to accept what is.

It's the experience
of feeling connected
with everything
that exists.

Hell,
    on the other hand,
           is s e p a r a t i o n.
  It's the experience of being
           d
            i
             s
               connected
from yourself and your inner guide.

It leads to selfishness
    and the desire to have things
      your own way,
      Instead of
      wanting what is best for all
          involved.

It's that feeling
    of C o N f U S i o N
      that comes when you do
  the same things over and over again
  and foolishly expect
      different results.

Wake up!

You're doing it again!

You think that
a new job,
a new relationship,
more money,
or something else outside of yourself
is what you need to make you happy.

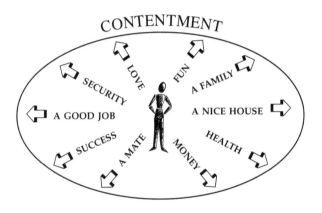

You'll never be content this way,
at least not for long.

You have to change your perspective,
change your approach,
and instead of searching for
contentment…

...Choose to be content first.

> *Then do what you need to do,*
> *and live life*
> *to its fullest.*

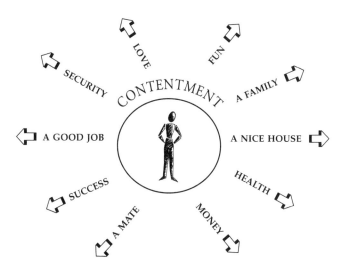

Contentment
>   *is*
>   *an*
>   *inside*
>   *job.*

> *To experience it,*
> *you must first learn to be at ease*
> *within your own skin*
> *and learn to be okay with what is.*

Accept this dream as a warning…

Wake up!

*If you don't,
the universe will wake you up,
and that's usually not a pleasant
experience.*

Trust me!

I awoke immediately after reading the last words: *"Trust me!"* which flashed in large, flaming red letters in my mind, tongues of fire extending from the body of each letter. I grabbed my journal to write down the dream, as well as the words in the dream book, and then I headed straight to Granddad's.

He was sitting on his front porch, rocking and listening to a radio when I arrived. Indian flute music filled the air.

"What's up?" he asked, as I walked up the steps to his porch.

"I had another dream, but then you already knew that, didn't you?"

"No, actually I didn't," he replied.

"You knew about the other dreams. How come you don't know about this one?"

"It's all a matter of focusing and tuning in. You don't think that I'm going to choose to tune into your station all of the time, do you? I tuned into you quite a bit when you first got here, but for the most part now, you're on your own. Sorry, but there are some mighty fine stations out there, so I changed the channel."

"You're talking in riddles again," I said, not understanding a word he was saying.

"Here, watch."

Granddad changed the station on the radio to a country station.

"I liked the flute music better," I said.

Then he turned it again, this time to an easy listening station. Next was a rock-n-roll station.

"David, you're like a radio, except you get to choose your own stations. This is what some people listen to," he said, as he turned the knob in between stations. Static hissed from the speakers... "Or this," he said, as he turned the knob rapidly from station to station. "These people can't focus on one thing. They want it all, which makes their minds fragmented and out of control."

"So we all choose what our life's about and what stations we want to hear," I replied.

"Yep, some tune into God, others to money and possessions, and some just hear static all day long. Others keep flipping the channels, unable to decide what they want, but fairly sure they want something different from what they've got. Life passes them by while they're trying to get what they want, trying to get it all done, or trying to figure it all out. They miss the little bits of heaven all around 'em."

"Little bits of heaven?" I asked.

"You know,... the beauty of an eagle soaring overhead... the colors of the leaves in fall... an ice cold drink on a hot summer's day... all are glimpses of heaven. For a runner, it might be finding that perfect stride on a cool spring morning; or for parents, it could be those few free moments of peace they have after the children are asleep.

"Personally," said Granddad, "I enjoy sitting here in my chair and doing nothing but being, or lying down on a Sunday afternoon with a cool spring breeze blowing through my bedroom window. The breeze gently lifts the curtains and softly touches my face; I lie there feeling totally appreciative of life and what it brings me. There's food in the house, a place to sleep, my friends and family are well, and there is nothing I have to do but enjoy gazing out the window. Everything is okay, just as it is. There's no resistance, no judgment, just an open awareness of the oneness of all things and my place in that oneness."

Then he looked me straight in the eye and said, "That is heaven – feeling totally open to what life is giving you."

"But how often does life get that perfect?" I asked. "It's not always springtime, and I rarely have nothing to do."

"Maybe I misled you by only mentioning the more obvious bits of heaven," replied Granddad, "but most people have to see those before they are ready, willing, and able to open to the others. Remember, heaven is where God is, and God is everywhere. Bits of heaven are all around us, and as you open up you will see them in places and at times you never thought possible before."

"But I'm not wanting bits of heaven now and then. I want it all the time, like you have it."

"And that you can have," he replied, "if you're willing to tune in to what is, instead of focusing on what could be... Close your eyes."

"Right now?"

"Yes, right now."

I followed his directions: "Take in a deep breath... Experience the air flowing in and the air flowing out... Become aware of your body... Notice how it feels... and accept what you feel as okay... Listen to the birds... Hear the sweetness of their songs... Breathe in your connection with all that is..."

After a few minutes, I could feel myself relaxing, and before long, all of the tension within me had faded away.

"Okay, now you can let your eyes slowly drift open," said Granddad, easing me out of my meditation. "Now your mind is clearer, and you have temporarily let go of your many wants and desires. How does it feel?"

"It feels good. I feel relaxed and at ease. But I'm not sure I can let go of everything like that for very long."

"And you don't need to. Just do it for a little while everyday. I usually do it in the morning, so that I can start the day fresh. I mentally and emotionally let go of everything. I temporarily let go of my friends, my family, my savings, my house, my truck, and even my good looks," he said with a twinkle in his eye. "It's much easier to start the day open and free than to try to get there later, once the craziness of the day has taken over."

"Still Granddad, I don't think I'm very good at letting go. I'm much better at holding on… but I'm willing to give it a try."

He nodded approval. "That sounds like a place to start. And if you can't do it at first, just stay open to the possibility, and it'll happen eventually. Don't fret about it. When you're ready to let go, you will."

I spent most of the morning at Granddad's talking in the yard. Afterwards, I stopped by Jenny's to visit with her and Alex awhile. Jenny was all excited about my spending so much time with Lynn at the party, and she couldn't hear enough of the details about our time together. Jenny thought it was great that I was meeting Lynn for church on Sunday, and she wanted me to give her a call or stop by the next day to let her know how it went.

I arrived at church Sunday morning to find Lynn sitting outside on a bench beside a magnificent, three-tiered fountain. The fountain was the centerpiece of a cozy, circular garden on the right side of the church. Lynn was dressed all in white. She looked like an angel. She was facing away from me, so she didn't see me approaching. I stopped to gaze at her for a few moments before walking up and saying, "Hi."

"Oh. Hi, David," she replied, as she gracefully turned my way.

"This is a beautiful garden," I said. "I bet it's even prettier in the spring time."

"Yes, it really is, but I love to sit here anytime of year." Then she stood and said, "I guess we better go on in and get ourselves a seat, don't you think?"

"Yeah, we might as well," I said.

"I sure did enjoy our talk the other night."

"Me, too," I replied.

"I hope you didn't think I was too forward in asking you to meet me for church."

"I was glad you did."

While we were walking to the front of the church, I found myself feeling uneasy. It was the same eerie feeling that I had experienced at the party – again, I felt I was being watched. Before we entered the building, I stopped to glance around. At first I didn't see anything unusual, but then I noticed a man in a white pick-up truck parked on the far side of the street. When I looked toward him, he turned away. I caught only a glimpse of his face, but he looked familiar. Still, I couldn't place him.

Lynn called to me, "David, is there something wrong?"

"No, it's nothing," I replied. "I just thought I saw someone I knew."

Upon entering the church, thoughts of the man in the truck faded away as my eyes and attention were drawn to the vibrant, stained glass windows set into the walls of the building. Each one told a story of Jesus. One depicted his healing of a sick man. Another portrayed his walking on the water. My favorite showed Jesus sitting in the midst of a group of children with a baby in his lap.

Lynn chose to sit in a pew near the back of the church, and I slid in beside her.

"I hope Reverend Thurman has a good message today," Lynn whispered to me, as we sat down. "He usually does."

"It will be fine," I said, reassuringly. Then I added, "I can't get over this building. I love the gothic architecture."

"Me, too," she replied. "There's a kind of mystical feeling about this place. I just like to sit here in the midst of it all."

It wasn't long before Reverend Thurman stood up and the service began. I glanced at the bulletin and was surprised to see the title of his talk, "A New Reality." This might be interesting, I thought to myself.

We sang some songs, prayed, had announcements, and then Reverend Thurman read a passage of scripture. The pre-sermon segments of the service didn't hold my attention very well, and my thoughts kept wandering back to the man in the pick-up truck who had been watching me as I entered the church. Suddenly, I realized where I had seen him before – he looked a lot like the man in my last dream. Both had dark hair and deep-set eyes. I pondered my realization, but I couldn't make any sense of the coincidence.

Reverend Thurman started his talk with the story of Jesus' walking on the water. As he spoke, my attention slowly shifted from interest in my new realization to interest in the message the Reverend was giving. He told us how afraid the disciples were when they saw something coming toward them on top of the water. Then they realized it was Jesus. He described Peter trying to walk out on the water to Jesus, and he said it was Peter's fear and lack of faith that made him sink.

"Jesus was trying to show Peter and the others a new reality," said Reverend Thurman. "Peter tried to accept the reality that Jesus was displaying, but he lost faith. He didn't lose faith in Jesus, however, as some people think. He knew who Jesus was, and he knew that Jesus could do amazing things. Peter lost faith in himself. He couldn't see himself living the reality that Jesus was modeling for him. He couldn't see himself doing the kinds of things that Jesus was able to do."

The rest of the talk was about Jesus' miracles and his statement that "he who believes in me will also do the works that I do, and greater works than these will he do."

Throughout the service, my mind kept comparing what the minister was saying with what Granddad and my dreams had been teaching me. I was surprised at the similarity between the three teachings.

Reverend Thurman ended his message by challenging the congregation, "Do you want to experience a new reality, or do you want to continue to live the limited life that you are presently living? It's your choice!"

When the service was over, Lynn turned to me and asked, "What'd you think?"

"I thought it was good," I replied.

"I thought so, too," she said with a smile.

Then we worked our way through the crowd, out of the church, and into the sunshine.

"Would you like to go get something to eat?" I asked.

"Sure."

"What are you in the mood for?"

She thought for a second and then answered, "There's a Mexican restaurant nearby."

"That's fine with me... Let's do that," I replied.

"Can I ride with you?"

"Yeah, come on."

It didn't take us long to get to the restaurant. We talked about the sermon while we waited for a table.

"What did you think about Reverend Thurman's 'new reality'?" asked Lynn.

"I think he's right," I replied, as I thought back to my talks with Granddad and my dreams. I wasn't sure how much of it to tell her. I decided to keep my sharing at a minimum, until we got to know each other better.

"His talk made me think back to my college days," said Lynn. "My girlfriends and I used to call ourselves the 'semi-normals,' because we didn't want to live a nine to five, rat race, kind of life. We didn't want to live the norm of two and a half children, a mortgage, a cat, a dog, and a house at the lake. We wanted something different, something more spiritual."

"Well, I guess I'm a 'semi-normal,' too, because I see things that way myself," I replied, which brought an approving grin to Lynn's face.

Just then the hostess walked up, showing us to our table.

"I'm starved," I said to Lynn. "What's good?"

Lynn recommended the taco salad, so that's what we both ordered. While we waited for our food, we continued our discussion.

"What do you think about miracles, David? Do you think they still happen like they did back in Jesus' day?"

"I think they happen," I replied. "Much of life seems a miracle to me."

"But I'm talking about miracles like Jesus did. You know, healing people, turning the water into wine, walking on water... things like that."

"Yeah, I think they happen."

"Have you ever seen one?"

"No, not like what Jesus did," I said, as our waitress placed our salads before us.

After we finished eating, I took Lynn back to the church to get her car. She paused before getting behind the wheel. "Would you call me tomorrow night? I'd love to hear how your first day on the job went."

I was thrilled. She seemed genuinely interested.

I headed home and found myself humming the "Twelve Days of Christmas": "...f i i i ive golden rings, four calling birds, three French hens, two turtle doves, and a partridge in a pear tree." It was an old habit of mine to sing Christmas tunes, "Zippity Doo Dah," or "Take Me Out to the Ball Game" when I was really happy or when it felt as though things were going my way. The time of year was irrelevant. I was known to sing Christmas songs even in the middle of an August heat wave.

4 New Habits

I woke up extra early Monday morning. I had planned an early start so that I would have time to meditate and become centered before my first day at school. The excitement of a new job and a new relationship made sitting still a challenge, but I stuck with it and eventually became reasonably calm.

I arrived at Fair Hope about forty-five minutes before I had to, finding a spot outside the dining hall to sit and get a feel for the place. It might be nice working here, I thought, as I gazed through the trees at the morning sun reflecting off Fair Hope's small lake. The morning dew on the grass, the brightness of the sun, the aged trees, and the light, foggy mist rising from the lake created a magical effect that brought images of elves and fairies to mind.

Fair Hope, like many adolescent treatment centers, had a community area which included a dining hall, a school, and office buildings. Not far away, were the cottages where the teenagers lived. All of the buildings were woodsy looking, some of them resembling log cabins.

It was a coed campus, two male cottages and two female cottages. There were forty teenagers in all, ten to a cottage. The teens ranged in age from thirteen to eighteen years old. They were at Fair Hope for all kinds of reasons. Many of them had been physically, emotionally, and/or sexually abused. Others were there because they had pushed the limits and had gotten into trouble with the courts.

My job was to help them prepare for life on their own. I was to teach them how to hunt for and keep a job, find an apartment, cook, manage their money, do comparative shopping, and all of the other things they might need to know to make it in life on their own.

My first day at work, I met with my supervisor and attended orientation classes. The classes were somewhat informative, but I was glad when the day was over. I had not come to Fair Hope to be a student; I was there to teach.

When I got home, I called Lynn. While we were on the phone, I asked her if she'd like to get together on the upcoming weekend, and she invited me to her apartment for dinner on Friday.

I spent the remainder of the first week of school reading client files, preparing classes, and getting to know a few of my co-workers. One teacher, Mr. Franklin, was a retired army lieutenant who was teaching so he could send his daughter through medical school. He spent all of his spare time fishing. I really liked him; he had a gentle but firm way about him.

The other teacher, Mrs. Tyson, was a bony middle-aged woman with long pink fingernails and hollow cheeks on each side of a beak-like nose. She reminded me of a vulture. She seemed to have a chip on her shoulder. I couldn't figure out what was beneath her anger. She didn't appear to like anything or anybody, and she seemed to openly dislike teenagers. I decided to keep her at a safe distance until I had a better understanding of what she was about.

And then there was my supervisor, Christine Banks, a stocky woman with short dark hair who appeared to be in her early forties. She looked straight-laced in her preppie polo shirts and khaki pants or skirt. But I was told she was quite colorful, often telling dirty jokes or stories and she was known to cuss now and then, too – traits she had picked up from from her late husband who had been in the navy.

But what impressed me most about Christine was her genuine love for the kids. You could hear it in her voice as she told stories about previous students. I also was impressed with her method of supervision. She was into empowering people, staff as well as kids.

My first week at Fair Hope was pleasant, though I would have liked it to have gone by faster. I could hardly wait to see Lynn on Friday night.

When I finally arrived at Lynn's, she was preparing spaghetti, and the aroma from the simmering sauce made me aware of how hungry I was. We drank a glass of wine, and I helped her make a salad while we waited for the sauce and noodles to finish cooking.

Lynn had a cozy, relaxed-looking apartment that made me think of the beach. She had shells scattered around for decorations, and the pictures on her walls showed scenes of harbors, boats, and beaches. Her furniture was all made of bamboo and wicker, and the cushions were colored in splashes of tan, green, and blue.

Dinner was wonderful, and Lynn surprised me by having banana pudding for dessert. I had mentioned how much I liked it during our conversation at the party. I was surprised and pleased that she had remembered, and I was touched by her taking the time to make it.

After dinner, Lynn asked me to play the guitar for her again. When I told her that my guitar was at home, she went into another room, coming back with a guitar case in hand. She said that she had started taking lessons a few months before, and she had bought herself a small Yamaha. I tuned her guitar, played a few songs and then asked her to show me what she had learned. Lynn was reluctant at first, but eventually she consented and played some for me.

"You'll be giving your own concerts before you know it," I commented when she had finished. "You're a natural."

"Thank you. But I think you're exaggerating just a bit," she replied.

"No, I'm serious. You're really good."

After we finished playing the guitar, Lynn offered to give me a back rub, "to pay me back for my performance." I smiled inwardly at her aggressiveness and accepted without hesitation. As I lay on the floor with Lynn rubbing my back, I thought about how well our relationship was going. I was so at ease when we were together.

Lynn must have massaged my back, arms, neck, and hands for twenty minutes before she stopped and said, "My turn."

We traded places. As I sat next to her rubbing her back and arms, I felt overwhelmed by her innocent beauty. Her hair was in a pony tail, which exposed the back of her neck. The wisps of hair on her neck looked so soft and pretty against her tanned skin.

Even though it had been only a week since we'd met, I felt that Lynn was the kind of woman I could marry. It was crazy thinking such thoughts, but that was how I felt.

When I finished her massage, Lynn rolled over on her back and looked up at me.

"That was great!" she said.

Her eyes gazed directly into mine, and I sensed that she was inviting a kiss. I looked deep into her eyes for what seemed like ages, and then slowly, I bent toward her until our lips touched. I was surprised at their softness. After a few moments, I again looked into her dancing, blue eyes. I caressed her cheek with the back of my fingers, and then I kissed her once more.

"You have the softest lips," I said.

She smiled, as she put her hand behind my head and gently drew me toward her. I lay my chest against hers. I could feel our hearts pounding. The longer we touched and kissed, the more our bodies seemed to mold together. And though part of me just wanted to let the passion take over, I wasn't sure that was the best thing to do; it felt too fast. I knew we'd better stop soon, or we would be unable to stop at all.

Inside of me a war was raging. The voice of my inner self was crying, "Slow down," while the voice of desire was urging me on, "Don't stop! Don't stop!" Finally, my inner self won out. I kissed her gently on the cheek and smiled at her.

"I wish I could have a massage like this everyday," I said, as I lay down beside her on the carpet.

"Me, too… but I don't know if we would appreciate them as much if we had them everyday," replied Lynn.

"You're probably right, but it would be a wonderful experiment."

"It *would* be nice," she agreed.

We lay there in silence for a few moments before Lynn said, "What do you want out of life, David?"

"What do you mean?" I asked.

"What's your vision of the rest of your life?"

"You're talking realistically, what I want to happen?"

"Yeah," she replied.

After a brief pause, I said, "Ever since my dad died, I've wanted to figure life out. I've often thought that we're missing the point of it all. I'd also like to get married some day and own my own home, nothing fancy, maybe a three bedroom brick house like my mom's. And of course, I want to teach."

"You really like teaching, don't you?"

"Yes, I've always enjoyed helping kids learn. Even in grammar school, I always helped the kids who had a hard time. What about you? What do you want?"

"I'm not sure. I know I want to get married and have children. Probably three or four children." She paused and then asked, "How about you? You didn't say anything about having children. Do you want to have kids?"

I knew it was a big question. I could see the anticipation in her eyes.

"I wouldn't mind having a few kids, though to be honest, I'd probably like to skip the diaper days and start with them about four to six years old, but yeah, kids are fine with me."

She pondered my answer for a few seconds before continuing, "I also would like to live on a golf course like I did growing up. I enjoyed being able to go to the driving range or practice putting whenever I wanted."

I was stunned. The prayer that I had said my first night at Jenny's rushed back into my mind.

"I didn't know you played golf," I replied, half dazed.

"Yeah, my father plays all the time. He started teaching me when I was five."

I barely heard a word she said. My mind kept comparing

Lynn with the prayer I had said just a few weeks before. She was about five foot two inches tall, had blue eyes, blond hair, and played golf and the guitar – just what I had asked for.

Then Lynn brought me back from my thoughts by asking, "Do you play?"

"Uh, yeah, I play," I replied. "Maybe we can play some time."

"I'm not very good. You'd probably get frustrated playing with me."

I kept the conversation going, but I was only half present. I had never had such an obvious answer to prayer, and it took me a while to get past the shock.

Though the events of Friday night were strange, it was not until the next evening that the really unusual things began to occur. Lynn and I were at my apartment lying on the floor watching a movie. I had just finished giving her a lengthy massage. As she was rolling over on her side she asked, "Do you know what time it is?"

"No, my watch is over on the coffee table," I replied. "But it's probably about 12:04."

After saying, "12:04," I wondered why I had been so specific instead of just saying about 12 o'clock.

Lynn glanced at my watch, and then she turned and stared at me with a strange look on her face.

"It's 12:04," she said. "How did you know that?" She looked around the room. "There aren't any clocks that you could see. Do you have two watches?"

"No, that's just what came to mind."

She didn't believe me, so she checked to see if I had another watch. Over the next couple of hours, Lynn tested me five times to see if I could do it again. Each time, magically, the correct time flashed in my mind: 12:23… 12:44… 1:01… 1:27… and 1:46. I was amazed. Lynn was not so happy, however. At first, she kept trying to figure out how I was doing it. Then she seemed wary and a little frightened, but by the fifth and final time, she had relaxed a bit. She said that maybe my knowing the time was just part of the new reality we had heard about the previous Sunday.

The next day, when I told Granddad about my new talent, he said, "That's good. It says you're opening up some… But your excitement concerns me. I don't want you to become focused on acquiring special powers and talents. That's ego stuff. Besides, what you did was not really that unusual anyhow. Synchronistic things like that happen to people everyday.

"Experiences like yours occur for one of two reasons. Sometimes they happen to lead people along their path, but much of the time they occur just to wake people up. Yes, and some people do develop extraordinary talents and powers. But focusing on such things is a big mistake.

"So when weird things like this happen, just smile at their occurrence, and then let 'em go. Don't let them distract you from your path."

*   *   *

When I awoke Monday morning, images of my incredible weekend with Lynn filled my mind. It wasn't long, however, before those images faded and I focused on the situation at hand – my first day of classes at Fair Hope.

With much anxiety and anticipation, I entered my classroom to wait for my students to arrive. My stomach was churning. I had a bad case of first day jitters. As I waited, hoping for a lively day of learning and getting to know each other, I tried to relax and calm myself. I let my eyes drift shut, focusing on my breath as it flowed in and out. In and out. In and out. In… and… out… in… and… out.

The first student to arrive was a light-skinned girl with a curly afro, who looked to be about thirteen or fourteen years old. She was wearing a gold top and white jeans, and she looked as if she had made a special effort to look nice for her first day of school.

"Good morning," I said, as she entered.

"Are you our new teacher?" she asked immediately.

"Yes ma'am, I am. I'm Mr. Harper… What's your name?"

"Tabitha Jones," she replied shyly.

As her name was leaving her lips, two long-haired teenage boys exploded onto the scene, the larger one chasing the smaller one and slapping him across the top of his head while yelling, "That's my little sister, and don't you touch her again."

They ran across the room knocking desks to the left and right out of their path. When they reached the far wall, the smaller boy ducked down, put his hands over his head, and screamed, "Stop it, you big ass hole!"

"Don't you be calling me no ass hole," the larger boy replied, as he kneed the smaller boy in the side. "I'll beat the shit outta you."

"Hold on there," I said, totally taken off guard and not sure what else to say.

The larger boy turned my way, and scowled, "And who the hell do you think you are?"

Tabitha quickly replied, "He's our new teacher."

"As if I give a shit," said the boy.

"You better listen to him," Tabitha continued.

"And if I don't?" challenged the boy.

Luckily, some of the other kids came in and things calmed down without my really having to handle the situation.

The first day was wild and woolly. It was a rough beginning, but after school, I felt fairly good about it. I had made some progress with my students, and as far as I could tell, I hadn't made any major mistakes.

I stopped by Granddad's to talk, but he wasn't there. When I got home I found an envelope with my name on it taped to the door of my apartment. The note said: "I'll be gone for a few days, but I'll be back late Friday evening. While I'm gone, I suggest that you take some time to listen inside for what you need to do next on your journey. Remember, your gut will show you the way, if you let it. Come by Saturday morning if you can, and let me know what you've come up with," signed Granddad.

After reading the note, I went for a long run. Then I meditated for a while. Some thirty minutes into my meditation my mind began to fill with thoughts of what I might do next on my journey. I spent the rest of the evening thinking and writing in my journal.

By the time Saturday morning arrived, I felt fairly pleased with what I planned to share with Granddad. After breakfast, I hopped into my new Camry and buzzed on over to his house. There was no answer when I knocked on the front door, so I headed around back. I felt certain that's where he would be.

As I rounded the corner, coming to the backyard, I stopped dead in my tracks. Granddad was sitting under the mimosa tree with his legs crossed and his eyes closed as before, but this time a bright red cardinal was perched on his left shoulder. Though I walked as quietly as I could, Granddad evidently heard me, opened his eyes and stretched. The cardinal flew away.

"How'd you do that?" I asked.

"What?"

"The cardinal," I said. "How did you get him to sit on your shoulder?"

"It's just a matter of trust,… just like the rest of life… But I think that's lesson number eighty-four, or is it number forty-eight? I can never remember," he said laughing, his eyes dancing mischievously. "Today, let's deal with lesson number three, or is it four? Anyway, did you figure out the next step in your adventure?"

"Maybe… I have some ideas."

"Let me hear 'em."

Still thinking about the cardinal, I mindlessly opened my journal to the things I had written and handed my notebook to Granddad. I had listed everything I could think of that might help me become a healthier, more spiritual person. I had made my list based on the idea that if my body and mind were pure and whole, then certainly my spirit would follow.

As Granddad read, I recalled what I had written:

- I will meditate twice daily for at least twenty minutes each time.
- I will exercise at least three to four times per week.

- I will make journal entries daily.
- I will quit eating meat and fatty foods.
- I will not eat sweets, and instead, I will eat more fruit.
- I will quit drinking coffee and tea.
- I will have a quiet time and read some in a
  spiritual book everyday.

I could hardly contain myself, waiting for his response. I felt like a man who had just asked a woman to marry him.

After a long silence, Granddad said, "You're pretty ambitious, aren't you?"

"Mom always taught me to do my best," I replied.

He chuckled. "That's exactly what *I* taught *her!* But I've acquired some new information since raising your mom. It's a shame God doesn't give every parent a manual on how to raise a healthy child, but I guess that's not the design. It would remove some of the adventure, wouldn't it?

"Anyway, doing your best and striving to achieve excellence are not always the best ways to live. Hard work and living right aren't all they're cracked up to be. There are other principles you can practice, which are much closer to the truth and which will help you live more abundantly. What is it you're hoping to accomplish by doing the things on your list?"

I thought for a few seconds, reaching into my thoughts for the goals I had written for Granddad just a week before. "I want to experience heaven," I replied, "and I figure that if my mind and body become healthier, that will help."

"There's some truth to that, but if it's heaven you want, you're going to need a different approach. Remember, you can't work your way into heaven, and more is not always better. In fact, the harder you work at achieving heavenly contentment, the less likely you are to experience it."

"Should I just throw my list away then?"

"It's not the list, David. You can be a vegetarian, if you want. It's a good thing, if you know how to do it correctly. I eat very little meat myself. And you're right, sugar's not good for you. But that's not the main issue. If you're focused on the shoulds and should nots of eating, or anything else for that matter, you'll spend much of your life preoccupied and possibly miss heaven altogether. Besides, as one becomes more physically and spiritually sensitive, one tends to eat better automatically without having to expend a whole lot of effort in doing so."

I felt disappointed. I thought my list was on target and would please Granddad. His reaction perplexed me. I shook my head and said, "Well then, I don't know where to start."

"You can start by not putting so much pressure on yourself. Having to eat a certain way, or be a certain way, will only create resistance within you. Then you'll want everything that you can't have, and the more you try to get rid of something, the more you'll want it."

"So what do I do? Just do whatever? And eat whatever I want?"

"Eat smart. You know what's good for you and what's not. Don't stuff yourself with sweets or eat pork everyday, but don't completely deny yourself either.

"If you find yourself torn between a grilled chicken sandwich and a bacon cheeseburger, choose the healthier one. If you want a candy bar once in a while, eat one, but don't be plagued by guilt as you eat it. Enjoy it! Sometimes we just need to treat ourselves for emotional reasons. Besides, the hassles we give ourselves about eating unhealthy foods are at least as bad for us as the food itself. Just eat the candy bar and visualize it nourishing you as it goes down."

"I like your approach, Granddad. I can eat whatever I like."

"That's not exactly what I said," he cautioned. "Eat healthier more often than not, but don't be rigid. Take the middle path of balance."

"Well, certainly you want me to meditate and exercise."

"I do, but even pursue those in moderation. We don't want to empty your mind of one agenda or obsession just to fill it with another. We're aiming to help you have a free, open, and creative mind: one that is flexible and able to perceive the truth; one that doesn't have to be entertained virtually every moment of everyday; one that is unhampered by fear and desire, and therefore, free to enjoy the heaven all around it."

"Granddad, I can't imagine such a mind. My mind has always been full, always trying to solve one problem or another and obsessed with doing everything just right."

"That's our challenge, helping you find new and better ways of occupying your mind, so that you can live a habit-free life. But for now, we'll settle for some new, healthier habits, the kind that lead to a more disciplined and focused, yet open and trusting sense of awareness."

"Sitting in meditation does that," I replied.

"Yes, meditation is an excellent place to start, but we want to move beyond just sitting. Let me see your journal."

In my journal he wrote:

1. *UNCONSCIOUSLY*
   UNAWARE

2. *CONSCIOUS OF*
   OUR LACK OF AWARENESS

3. *CONSCIOUSLY*
   AWARE

4. *SUPER CONSCIOUSLY AWARE*
   AND IN THE FLOW

As he showed me what he had written, he said, "This is the progression we go through in moving toward spiritual awareness and wholeness. There are four steps. First, we begin unconsciously unaware. We walk around asleep and don't even realize it. Then, something happens that wakes us up to how unaware we really are. That's the beginning of step two, and the search for awareness and truth begins. Often times, at this point, we start to explore ways to become more aware."

"That's where I am," I responded.

"It's difficult to say for sure where someone is along the path. You're probably right, though.

"Then, in the third stage, our consciousness begins to grow and develop and we find the path of openness and trust. After we live in that state for a while, it becomes a part of us, and we begin to see things in a whole new light. Then one day, we reach stage four and move beyond normal consciousness and what most people think is reality into the real adventure, a free flowing super consciousness."

"I wish it didn't take so long." There was my impatience again.

"For some people, it doesn't. There are those who become enlightened all at once. Most, however, go through a process of realization. First, they realize the truth in their head, and eventually it shifts into their being, but even then, the first big enlightenment experiences they have usually feel so powerful that they think they have just had an instant awakening."

"But Granddad, meditating so much… isn't that kind of self-absorbed and self-centered?" I asked. "Jesus said we need to lose ourselves, not focus on ourselves."

"Good point. That's true. But you have to find yourself before you can lose yourself. Right now, you are just a bunch of resistance and reactions in human form, and until you realize the truth of who you are, that's all you'll ever be. Right now, if someone puts you down, don't you react with anger? If they praise you, you react by blushing or smiling, and you feel all warm inside. Much of your life is a reaction to others' critiques and expectations of you."

"Everybody does that; it's just part of life," I replied, defensively.

"Not everyone. That's not how I live."

I felt confused and I sat back at a loss for words. Finally, I said, "That's the only way I know. What's the alternative?"

"To learn to act instead of react. To become mindful and to learn to see yourself as you deal with a person or a situation, so that you can adjust as you go, instead of just reacting in an unhealthy way."

"Sounds schizophrenic and like a lot of work."

"Only if you are doing it along with a million other things all at once. When you can slow down your life and do one thing at a time, it becomes quite easy."

"But I'm good at doing more than one thing at a time," I said proudly. "I used to take notes and write papers during class, sometimes keeping a journal at the same time, as well. And I used to dictate term papers while driving home for the weekend. It seemed like a waste of time to just drive for so long. To me, doing only one thing at a time doesn't seem like a very efficient way to live."

"Actually, it's more efficient," said Granddad. "It's all but impossible to relax and enjoy life while doing a bunch of things at once. You have to learn to set priorities and let the less important things go."

"I'm not sure I'm ready to do that yet, Granddad."

"I know; you want it all, like most everyone else does."

"No, not everything. But yes, there are certain things I want."

"David, do you know anyone who has it all? Or let me make that easier. Do you know anyone who has all they want?"

I pondered his question, and I realized that I didn't know anyone who had everything they wanted, except maybe Granddad.

"Only you," I replied, a bit stunned. It was a sobering realization. Maybe having all I wanted wasn't really possible.

"And how did I accomplish such a feat?" Granddad asked.

"That's what I'm trying to find out," I replied.

"Well, I'll tell you. But I'm not sure how much difference it'll make until you're ready to make some changes. The path to getting all that you want goes directly through emptiness. You have to let go of desire, let go of wanting, and let go of your need to have a life full of distractions. As soon as you do, you automatically have everything you want. Think about it. I know it sounds crazy and paradoxical, but that's the way it is.

"David, you can keep to your old ways, if you want. But if you want a new life, you have to come up with a new approach. It's up to you, but remember, only crazy people do the same things over and over again and expect different results… Are you crazy?"

"No."

"Good!" he said, patting me on the back.

As I drove home from Granddad's that day, I continued to ponder the things he had said. Though much of it made sense, his thought processes were still somewhat foreign to me. I had a feeling it was going to take me quite awhile to really grasp all that Granddad was trying to teach me.

5 Lessons from the Universe

By the middle of my third week of teaching school, I was wondering if my classroom would ever settle down and if I had made the right decision to come to Fair Hope. I was feeling more like a policeman or a babysitter than a teacher.

School aside, the rest of my life was flowing along rather well, other than feeling I was being watched every now and then. But I hadn't seen the man in the pick-up anymore. I was enjoying my talks with Granddad and learning about things that I had always wanted to know. And Lynn and I were seeing more and more of each other. We had started eating supper together a couple of nights a week, and we were spending most of our weekends together as well. We even played a couple of rounds of golf. Lynn was a much better golfer than she had let on. In fact, she beat me one day, which really pleased her. It gave her bragging rights, which she exhausted to the limit, saying things like, "I can't believe it, David Harper got beaten by a girl. What would his friends back home think about that?" I couldn't do anything except laugh with her. She had beaten me fair and square.

The longer we were together, the more Lynn and I found we had in common. We both had an abundance of energy and enjoyed having a good time. We loved to talk and could talk about anything and everything, and we did.

Lynn also seemed to admire and look up to me, which felt good. She thought that I had my life together, and she liked that. She seemed comforted by the fact that I had been to seminary, and she often wanted to know my opinion about spiritual questions that she had. I couldn't imagine finding anyone more right for me than Lynn.

As the days passed, my relationship with Lynn kept improving while my experience at school kept getting worse. By the middle of my fourth week, I was seriously wondering if working with troubled kids was the job for me. My classroom was still out of control, and precious little teaching happened each day. Some of the teenagers wanted to learn, but I was spending all of my time dealing with the misbehavior of the ones who didn't seem to care or didn't want to be at school in the first place. Several loved being disruptive; the worst one was Eric. He was the same boy who had challenged me on the first day of school.

He was big for his age and he intimidated others. He interrupted repeatedly so that I felt I had to teach over his noise and around him. The class would have been much easier without Eric.

He came into class this day with his usual swagger. He was wearing a button shirt, unbuttoned to the waist. He sat on top of his desk instead of in his chair.

My curriculum called for a broad review of money – from comparative shopping to making change and budgeting. Budgeting always brought Granddad to mind since rule one was putting the most essential things first. As I started talking, Eric started banging on his desk as if it were a set of drums. Some of the other students rolled their eyes at him. One said, "Cut it out," but Eric just got louder.

I asked him a couple of times to stop drumming and to get off his desk, but he paid me no attention. Finally his disrespect got to me, and I yelled, "Cut out the noise. Button your shirt. We don't want to see your chest! And get off that desk."

He grinned foolishly and pretended he was hitting a set of cymbals, "Cha-ching."

I lost it. How could I teach with this *idiot* disturbing everyone. I yelled, "Get outta here! Go down to the office!... NOW!"

Still grinning, he shrugged his shoulders, pulled his shirt

wide open, exposing his nipples, and sashayed out the door.

It was a relief to be rid of him. But minutes later, I spied him outside, loitering under a tree, looking toward the class windows with a grin. He had never even gone near the office. I was furious at the little punk. One of the girls giggled and said, "Hey Mr. Harper... your face is turnin' red!"

My life was getting way out of balance. I had been spending so much time with Lynn, there wasn't time for much else – not even meditation. I was losing touch with my path. I'd forgotten the list of goals I'd written and shown Granddad. I had to take action, and I decided to start with school. I asked Christine for a conference. We set one up for the following morning.

That night, I lay awake for hours pondering my situation. I didn't want Christine to think that I couldn't handle my students, but that was pretty much the truth of the matter.

When sleep finally took over, I found myself in the midst of another strange dream. I was walking through an alley between two large buildings. It was very foggy, and I couldn't see anything in front of me. I walked slowly, feeling my way as I went, eventually coming to the edge of the buildings and then stepping from the alley into the bright sunshine. There, I saw kids playing ball on a city street. They appeared to be about thirteen to sixteen years old, about the same age as my kids at school.

One of the boys missed the ball and ran to get it. While he was retrieving the ball, a car suddenly appeared from around a corner and ran over him. My mouth flew open in horror. I didn't know what to do. The other kids ran to get the ball, then returned to their play as if nothing had happened. They were totally unaffected by the accident.

Amazed, I ran toward them, yelling, "Why don't you help him?"

They answered, "Why? There are dead kids everywhere."

Sure enough, when I looked around, there were dead bodies all over the place – hundreds of them. Appalled, I stood in silence.

Then I noticed a figure with white hair and beard, dressed in a white flowing gown, floating in from the west. He resembled the pictures of Moses in my childhood Sunday school books.

I ran up to him and said, "Why don't you help these kids?"

And in a strong, deep voice, he replied, "WHY DON'T YOU?" and then he disappeared.

Suddenly, the scene changed, and I saw myself sitting on the steps of one of the buildings with the kids who had been playing ball sitting all around me. It appeared that I was speaking to them. I strained to hear what I was saying, but I couldn't hear anything.

Then Granddad and his two companions in white appeared and handed me the large, golden book. I opened the book and read:

You are right where you belong.

Let go of your doubts and fears,
and
trust the process.

Balance is the key.

Don't
let
your
doing
get ahead of your being.

Listen within,
and open to the truth.

It's all around you.

You see reality not as it is,
but as you have been taught to see it.

Only when you can let go of your old
perceptual filters,
your obsessions, your agendas,
and your resistance,
as well as good and evil,
will you truly be able to see.

Let go!!!

*T*here is really no such thing
as a good or bad event.

That may be difficult to believe,
but it's true.

*E*verything just is.

*I*t's your judgment that creates the
positive and negative feelings.

*F*or example:
Pain
is neither
good nor bad,
though it may be unpleasant.

Pain is a teacher,
a teacher of compassion.

It is also a warning,
a warning that something is out of balance.

Pain occurs when change is needed.

Don't resist pain.
Instead, listen to it,
sit with it,
accept it,
and soon
you will experience harmony.

Trust
will show you the way.

It alone
is able to open the door to heaven.

In fact,
you can measure
your spiritual growth
by your capacity to
trust the source of your being,
the universe,
and
the process of your own life.

When I awoke, my mind struggled to understand one question: Why couldn't I hear the discussion between the kids and myself? It didn't make sense. And it wouldn't make sense, until a few hours later.

Upon arriving at school that morning, I went straight to Christine's office for our conference.

"Christine," I said, "Are you ready for me?"

"Come on in. Have a seat," she replied, standing up from behind her desk.

Her reading glasses sat low on her nose, and she looked over them, watching me enter the room.

Her office was an inviting place, with pictures of unicorns, rainbows, castles, and clowns. Her bookshelves stored volumes of material on education and psychology, as well as dozens of knickknacks and figurines of fairies, wizards, and other mythical creatures.

The left side of her office housed a reddish-brown, oak desk that looked more like a decoration than a work place. Her desk was the picture of perfect order; everything seemed to be in its proper place. Her diplomas graced the wall behind it. The right side of the office was a sitting area with two oak rocking chairs and a comfortable sofa. I sat in one of the rockers and Christine sat in the other.

"How's it going?" she asked, as we sat down.

"Fairly well, I guess. No… not really. I feel like I'm in a battle for control of my classroom and the kids are winning."

"I know that doesn't feel good," she replied.

"No, it doesn't… I can't seem to get much teaching done. Mostly I've been dealing with misbehavior." I told her about Eric and the misbehavior of some of the other students. She sat quietly and listened.

After I finished, she said, "So you think having more control is the answer."

"Yes ma'am… Don't you?"

"Well, actually… No, I don't."

"I don't understand," I answered, stunned by her reply.

"Why struggle for control? They aren't going to give it to you anyway," she said. "They may comply, but that's not going to do them much good in the long run. Why not become an ally and share the control?"

"They would take over if I did that."

"Would they?… Have you tried it?"

I felt confused.

Christine continued, "Sometimes, we feel we need to do one thing, when actually, we need to do the opposite. When you feel you want to strangle one of these little cherubs, that often means that they need more attention, maybe even a hug. When you can't get them to listen to you, that usually means you need to listen to them. And when you feel the need for control, that's probably a clue that you need to give up some control."

She might as well have been speaking Russian. None of what she said made sense to me. "I'm not sure I'm following you," I replied.

"These students don't need an iron hand, David... nor a free hand, for that matter. They need boundaries, acceptance, empathy, and understanding. They don't need someone to lead them. They need someone to walk beside them, someone who teaches by example, rather than just with words. They don't need a teacher trying to fix their lives and give them all the answers, but a teacher who will help them find answers for themselves. How else are they going to learn to walk on their own and make it when they leave here, and we're not around?

"And remember, it's not your words that will make the difference. If you make a difference, it will be through your presence and what you model in your actions. If you want respect, you have to model respect. If you want control and power, you must give control and power to them."

My dream flashed back into my mind. Suddenly, I knew why I couldn't hear myself talking to the kids; words weren't important. It was one's presence that made the difference.

Christine continued, "These teenagers are trying to find their way. They're not afraid of you, so you can't intimidate them. What could you do to them that is anywhere near as bad as what they've already experienced? Many of them have been abused beyond what you and I can imagine.

"They will resist you every step of the way until they trust you and know that you trust them. They will be your adversaries until you show them that you're on their side, that you're an ally."

"You're saying that I should trust them to lead the way in their own learning when I can't even trust them to go to the bathroom without creating trouble?"

"I'm not saying you *should do* anything, but you can try it if you want. You will still have to facilitate the process by stepping in here and there for safety reasons. They also need help seeing their options and sometimes they need a mediator. But you don't have to feel the burden of their actions. Remember, when these kids screw up, it's not your fault. Likewise, it's not your victory when they do well. You have an impact on them, but they are responsible for their own lives, not you."

I felt a weight lifted from my shoulders. I had been judging my worth by their actions, and now I was beginning to see my job in a new light. Teaching was not about having all of the answers nor was it about fixing other people's problems.

"Christine, I like what you're saying, but I don't know how to make it practical for the classroom."

"You have to experiment," she replied, "and open up your creativity. I have some books that might help you get started. It's kind of like being a comedian; sometimes you have to tell some bad jokes and make some mistakes before you find a few good jokes that work for you. Not everything you try will be a success."

"But I have a curriculum to follow, remember?"

"That's true; there are certain things you must teach, but you have quite a bit of freedom in how you go about teaching them."

"I wish I could see someone do what you're talking about."

"You think that would help? Would you like to watch me teach your class one day?" she asked.

"Would you?"

"Sure, no problem."

"When?"

"How about today?" she replied.

"You don't need time to prepare?"

"Not much. I'm going to let them choose what we do, anyway."

I was doubtful but curious, so I took Christine up on her offer. She modeled her words to the tee, letting them choose the topics for the day from my curriculum, and then she used their creativity, as well as her own, to make it fun.

For the first hour and a half, my students behaved well for her. I figured they were behaving because she was the coordinator of the school. Then some of their normal behavior began to surface. Christine was undaunted by anything they did. She calmly handled each disturbance by calling on the student's sense of fairness, by setting boundaries, by giving choices, and by calling on the group's support. As I watched her work her magic, I realized that I had a lot to learn, and that Fair Hope was exactly where I needed to be.

By the end of the day, I was in total awe of Christine Banks. In one day, she had taken my class of rebellious, loud-mouthed teenagers and turned them into excited students who were open to learning.

The next day, I arose early to be sure I made time for meditation. I was excited about trying Christine's method of teaching and so it was difficult to center myself, but finally I did.

Though things only went about half as well as they did for Christine, it was still my best day yet. To celebrate, I asked Granddad, Jenny, and Alex over for dinner. With work and Lynn taking up so much of my time and energy, I had seen little of them over the last month. Lynn volunteered to help me cook, which was a good thing, because cooking was definitely not my forte. I grilled the chicken and peeled the potatoes, and Lynn prepared the green bean casserole and the corn and mashed the potatoes.

We ate and talked for almost an hour. I felt like a grandmother, checking to see that everyone cleaned his or her plate, which they did.

After dinner, Jenny and Lynn went out on the balcony to talk. Granddad and I entertained Alex for a while with a game of hide-and-seek in my apartment before joining the women outside. By the time we got out there, Jenny and Lynn were in a deep discussion, so we quietly pulled up chairs and listened.

"It's just not fair," Jenny said. "She's only four years old."

"No, it's not fair," Lynn replied. "It's easier to take when it's an older person. But when it's a child…" She stopped in midsentence as if she didn't know what else to say.

I didn't have any idea what they were discussing, but I could tell they were both disturbed.

"Sometimes life doesn't make any sense," said Lynn.

"You're right about that," said Jenny.

"What are y'all talking about?" I asked finally.

Neither of them spoke at first, and then Jenny said, "One of the girls in Alex's class has leukemia, and it's becoming obvious that the treatment is not working. She's just four years old." Jenny paused and then added, "It's not fair. It's just not fair."

"Who, Mom?" asked Alex.

"You know, little Beverly's been sick and hasn't been at school."

"Oh," he said, lowering his head.

"Beverly's one of Alex's best friends," Jenny told the rest of us.

I felt a great heaviness come over me, and my thoughts turned to my dad.

Jenny continued, "The family is torn up about it. I don't know what to say to Sue, Beverly's mother. What do you say to someone whose four-year-old child is dying?"

The silence was deafening.

"I don't know," I replied. "There's not much you can say."

"And where's God when something like this is happening?" Jenny asked, with anger in her voice.

"All I know to say is that God knows best," answered Lynn. "We just have to trust Him."

"Well that may be so," said Jenny, her eyes flashing wildly, "but I don't know if I can trust in a God who hurts four-year-old children."

Everyone was quiet, and then Jenny started to cry. I put my arm around her, and she put her head on my shoulder.

While I was holding her, Alex walked over to us. He put his hand on Jenny's knee, saying, "Mama, don't cry." Then tears began to roll down his cheeks, too.

Jenny pulled away from me, picked Alex up in her lap, and hugged him tightly. She began to rock him slowly back and forth.

"I love you," she said to Alex. "You're Mama's heart."

"I love you, too, Mama," Alex replied, between sobs.

After a few moments, Lynn said to Jenny, "I didn't mean to make you angry, Jenny."

"It's not you. I'm angry about the situation."

No one replied, and that was how the conversation ended. Jenny and Alex didn't stay much longer, and Granddad left when they did. I was perplexed at Granddad's silence during the discussion and planned to ask him about it later.

Lynn stayed to help me clean up the dishes, which we did in silence. Then, just as we were putting the last ones away, the phone rang.

I said, "Hello."

An angry male voice on the other end said, "I *know* you've been seeing *my* Lynn and that she's *there* with you right now. You keep seeing her and you're dead! This isn't a threat, it's a promise." Then he slammed down the phone.

My spine tingled and I could feel the color draining from my face.

Lynn asked, "What's wrong? Are you okay?"

"That was a death threat."

"A death threat!"

"Some guy said that if I continued to see you, he would kill me."

Lynn looked concerned. "What did he sound like?"

"He had a deep, country sounding voice... Do you know who it might be?" I asked.

"I'm not sure, but it sounds like Brian."

"Who's Brian?"

"A guy I dated about six months ago. I met him at church. He seemed really sweet at first, but after we went out a couple of times, he became very possessive."

"This guy sounded pretty possessive, all right. He called you *his* Lynn."

"That's probably who it is, then, because he has said that before."

"What's he like?"

"He's paranoid. He didn't want me to talk to anyone, girls included. He was afraid I would start dating someone else.

"He bought me real expensive gifts, and when I refused to take them, he insisted that I accept. He bought me that table in my dining room, that chest by the window, and even a diamond ring – all within the short two months we dated. I didn't accept the ring. It was the clincher that made me know he was crazy.

"When I quit seeing him, he called me four or five times every day for over two months. I talked with him some a few times, but then I let the answering machine handle his calls. He hasn't called for over three months now."

"He sounds crazy," I said. "Maybe even crazy enough to come after me, huh? Or do you think he's just bluffing?"

"I don't think he'd come after you," she replied, "but I don't know. We weren't around each other for very long. He didn't ever threaten to hurt me. In fact, Brian seemed very gentle at first, but his anger was just beneath the surface. It didn't take long for it to show up, but he never became physical."

"What does he look like?"

"He's big. He's well over six feet tall, and he weighs at least two hundred pounds. He has black hair that he parts in the middle and he has brown deep-set eyes… And he wears nice clothes."

As Lynn described Brian, my mind flashed back to that day at church when I realized that the man watching us as we entered the church looked a lot like the man in my dream. I couldn't be sure, but I had a feeling that Brian and the man in the white pick-up were one and the same. I told Lynn what I suspected.

"Yeah, I bet it is him," she replied. "He does drive a white pick-up." Then she paused before saying, "I'm sorry all of this is happening. Even though it's not my fault, I feel responsible."

"You're right; it's not your fault," I responded, as I pulled her close to me and kissed her on her forehead. "I don't want you feeling bad about this. He probably won't try anything any-way."

"I'm surprised that Brian would do this. I'm actually stunned. I figured that since I hadn't heard anything from him in more than three months, he had gotten over me."

Tears welled in her eyes and she said, "I want you to be care-ful. I couldn't stand it if something happened to you because of me. Maybe we shouldn't see each other for a while."

"Is that what you want?" I asked.

"No, but I don't want you to get hurt."

"Lynn, I don't want this to come between us. We have something special, and we don't need to change anything because of this. That's what he wants. The odds are he's just bluffing, and I'm willing to take my chances." I sounded a lot calmer than I felt. It was unnerving to have a threatening call and now I knew that he was big and mentally off balance.

"What about the police?" she said. "We could call them and see if they can do anything."

"I thought about that, but it probably wouldn't do any good. I'm not sure the police could really do anything anyway. And we're not absolutely sure that it was Brian who made the call."

We talked awhile longer, and then I walked Lynn out to her car. It took me a long time to fall asleep that night.

6 Good Luck? Bad Luck?

When I prepared to leave my apartment the next morning, I scanned the hallway before stepping out the door. My shoulders were tense and my stomach was in knots as I walked down the steps and out of the building. Hurrying to my car, I surveyed the surrounding area looking for anything unusual that might tip me off about an attack. I glanced in the back seat of the car before getting in to insure no one was hiding there. As I locked the doors, a big sigh of relief escaped me.

Driving down the street, I could feel my adrenalin pumping, preparing my body for any possible dangers I might encounter. Every few seconds, I checked my rearview mirror to make sure no one was following me. For the first few miles, I scanned every face in every car, as well as the faces of the pedestrians along the way. Then I came to my senses.

"This guy's not going to kill me this morning," I said to myself. He said that he would do it if I didn't quit seeing Lynn. He will, at least, give me a chance to quit seeing her. With this realization came a feeling of relief. I could feel my body begin to relax; the tension flowed from my face and shoulders. I was even able to laugh at myself a bit.

I decided not to tell anyone at school about the threat. There was no reason to create any unnecessary stir.

As the day wore on and I became more involved with the kids, thoughts of the threat completely left my mind. But when it was time to drive home, the presence of the threat returned. On the way home, I searched through faces once more.

I called Lynn soon after entering my apartment to let her know about my day and that I was okay. We decided to eat together at her place the following evening.

The next morning's drive to school was not much better than the previous day's trip, but like the day before, the chaos of school helped me escape the bad feelings. Driving to Lynn's that evening was quite another story, however; I felt as though everyone was watching me. This feeling became especially strong as I walked from my car to Lynn's door. I thought I saw movement behind the large bushes at the corner of one of the buildings. It was probably just a dog or cat. Still, I took the steps two at a time, racing to the safety of Lynn's apartment.

Lynn greeted me with a kiss and a hug.

"How are you doing?" she asked.

"Fairly well," I replied, "Though I'm a bit jumpy, to say the least."

"I thought about you all day, hoping you were okay, and hoping that it was all just a bluff."

"Yeah, I hope it was, too."

I followed Lynn into the kitchen to help her finish making dinner.

"This is a strange experience, dealing with the possibility of an attack," I said as I cut up a carrot for the salad. "It's made me think a lot about dying."

"I know. I've thought about that, too," she replied.

"I've been taking life for granted, and I'm not going to do that anymore. We never know how long we've got on this earth. I'm beginning to realize how much of my life I've wasted worrying about things that aren't really important."

Lynn listened quietly and then kissed me on the cheek.

Dinner was superb, and so was the rest of the evening, even though Lynn and I were both unusually quiet. We did talk some as we ate, but we were relatively silent afterwards. She gave me a long, forty-five minute body massage, and I returned the favor.

But as with school, the temporary reprieve from thoughts of the threat was just that, temporary, and before long it was time to go home. Riding in a car and entering my empty apartment had become a nightmare to me. I became extremely nervous at the thought of being out in the open and having to walk into my dark apartment.

As I left Lynn's that night, I again found myself imagining that someone was watching me. Feeling afraid, yet scoffing at my paranoia at the same time, I crossed the lot to my car. As I reached it, a truck slowly rounded the corner and came toward me. I hurried to get in. But I couldn't fit the key in the key hole. After what seemed like forever, the key finally went in. I quickly opened the door and slid in. The truck passed by just as I was closing the door behind me. I sighed in relief, but as the sigh left my mouth, a loud noise rang in my ears. It sounded like a gun shot. I dove across the car seat. I felt a sharp pain in my side as my head hit the seat cushion on the passenger side. Wondering if I'd been shot, I lay there motionless. Slowly, I moved my hand to my side to check the damage. Instead of blood and a bullet hole, I found the emergency brake protruding up between the seats into my side. Relieved, I shifted my body to ease the pain.

But what of the gunshot? I fearfully peeked out the window, but all I saw was the truck rounding another corner. There was a second resounding bang, and a few smaller ones following it. I ducked again, but this time I was careful not to dive across the emergency brake.

There were a couple more popping sounds, and I realized that the bangs were not gunshots after all. The truck was back-firing. Relieved, but feeling foolish, I sat up in the seat. My side was throbbing. I glanced in the direction of Lynn's apartment to see her running toward me.

Even though the windows of my car were up, I could hear her screaming, "Are you all right? Are you all right?"

I rolled down the window. "It was just a truck backfiring," I said, "but it gave me a scare, too."

"I thought it was a gun shot," she said, out of breath from running. "It scared me to death. I'm glad you're okay."

"You and me both!"

"You drive carefully, and call me when you get home so I'll know you made it safely. I won't be able to sleep if you don't call," she said, as she reached through the window to give me a kiss.

While driving home, I was struck by the irony that rather than our growing apart because of the threat, Lynn and I had actually become closer and more appreciative of one another. That thought made me smile in spite of my fearful ride home.

Once in my apartment, I carefully checked all closets and possible hiding places for intruders before sitting down on the sofa with my guitar to relax before bed. I hadn't been sitting there long when the phone rang. It was Lynn checking to see that I had made it home safely. I had forgotten to call her as I had promised. Almost immediately after I hung up, the phone rang again. I figured that it was Lynn and that she had forgotten to tell me something, but the voice on the other end was not pleasant this time.

"I warned you, and you didn't listen. Now you're going to have to pay!" said the angry voice… and hung up.

I began to tremble. My heart raced. I quickly checked all doors and windows to make sure they were locked. Every little sound sent a burst of adrenalin rushing through my body. I didn't get to sleep until around three in the morning, and even then, it wasn't a peaceful sleep.

Fear followed me all the next day. Even at work, I no longer felt safe. I found myself constantly searching for assassins. Being on edge and not quite myself, I became easily agitated, getting after the kids for things that wouldn't have bothered me before. I couldn't think clearly, and my creativity and ability to improvise vanished. By the end of the day, I was a worn out wreck, and I felt totally defeated.

There was no sign of Brian on the way home, but as soon as I opened my apartment door, I knew he had been there. My beautiful apartment was in a shambles. The kitchen cabinets had been cleaned out, and dishes, silverware, pots and pans were strewn everywhere. My closets, too, had been emptied, and my clothes littered the floor. There were no pictures left on the walls, and all of my furniture had been moved. It was a disaster. Since the balcony door was left open, I assumed that was how he had gotten in.

I felt violated and enraged. But my fear was gone. I was no longer going to sit back and wait for this guy to decide my fate. First I called the police. They came over to examine my apartment and look for fingerprints. I told them about the threats, but they said there was not much they could do until we could definitely identify the perpetrator.

Next, I tried to call Granddad to get his thoughts on the matter, but he wasn't home. Finally, I decided to take things into my own hands. It wasn't as if I was totally defenseless, anyway. I knew something about protecting myself. I had taken three years of aikido, a form of martial arts training, while I was in high school and one year while I was in seminary, but I hadn't attended any classes since graduating from seminary in May. There had been so much going on since moving that I hadn't even considered starting back yet. Now it was time. Even though I was just a brown belt, with a couple of years of training left before I could test for my black belt, I was proficient enough to protect myself to some degree, as long as my opponent was not carrying a gun.

I got out the yellow pages to look up aikido. There was only one school listed in the book, so I gave them a call. Their next class met on Saturday morning. I could hardly wait.

Being proactive instead of sitting back and waiting in fear made me feel stronger and affected my whole life in a positive way. The rest of my week went fairly well. My creativity came back, and school returned to normal. I even rested better at night. I still scanned for assassins, but I did so aggressively, rather than fearfully.

When I arrived at the aikido class Saturday morning, I found twelve people sitting around stretching and talking. There was a feeling of confidence emanating from the group. There were nine men and three women, ten of whom were wearing hakamas, the loose-fitting pants typically worn by those practicing aikido. Two of the men wore regular street clothes. They were probably newcomers. I wore sweat pants and a T-shirt. I had a hakama, but I didn't really like wearing it.

Most of the students seemed to be between twenty-five and fifty years old, but there were a couple of teenagers and one man who looked to be in his sixties. It was clear which person in the group was the instructor. He was a wiry-looking Asian man, a bit smaller than myself. He walked as one who feared nothing, yet there was a humble, reserved quality about him as well. He seemed at peace with himself which made him easily approachable. I liked him immediately. Judging from his graying hair and the wrinkles around his eyes, I guessed that he was in his mid-to-late forties.

"Hi, I'm David Harper," I said, introducing myself. "I'm interested in possibly taking aikido here."

"Hi, David," the man replied in a soothing tone. He had a distinct Asian accent, but he spoke perfect English. "Your voice sounds familiar. Did we talk on the phone recently?"

"Yes, Sensei. I called the other day." I was surprised and impressed that he remembered speaking with me.

"I'm Tsukuru Kuhara. I'm the chief sensei here. We would be glad to have you. Why don't you take off your shoes and join the others stretching. Have you ever taken aikido or any other martial arts?"

"Yes, Sensei, I've taken four years of aikido," I answered proudly.

"Good," he said. "Go stretch, and we'll talk some after class. The first session is on me. We'll talk about the cost of future classes later."

After a few minutes of stretching, Kuhara Sensei asked everybody to gather around him in a semi-circle. He waited for everyone to become still before he spoke.

"We have some new students with us today, so I want to take a few moments to talk about what we're doing here and what aikido is all about.

"Each of you has come to this class for a reason. Many people begin taking aikido in an effort to learn how to protect themselves, and that's fine. However, after taking aikido for a while, most of you will realize that these classes are about much more than just physically protecting yourself.

"Aikido is a way of being. As an aikido student, you will not only learn how to protect yourself but also how to avoid the need to protect yourself. You will learn about balance, and you'll learn how to find peace within yourself."

As he spoke, I could tell that Kuhara Sensei had depth, and I had a feeling that I was going to learn a lot from him. My previous instructors had been proficient in the physical techniques, but I had been disappointed in their lack of interest in the philosophy behind the techniques.

Sensei continued, "We reach peace by becoming one with ourselves and all that is around us. We become one by connecting with ki. Ki is the life force that is in, under, and through all that is. Reaching unity with ki is like becoming one with God's universe and God's essence. That is what we're all about here.

"When we are able to experience oneness with all that is, we will have no enemies. There will be no struggles and no need for the physical techniques you're going to learn."

He showed us the primary stance used in aikido and explained how such a stance was more balanced than other stances. He said that physical, emotional, and spiritual balance is essential to one who wished to tap into ki. When he spoke of ki, he sometimes touched his stomach. He said that ki enters one's body just above the navel. That was interesting to me, in light of all that I had learned from Granddad and my dreams. I wondered if there was a connection between Granddad's "gut" and Sensei's "ki," or if it was just a coincidence that both affected the same area.

Kuhara Sensei said, "When one learns to use ki, one becomes virtually immovable and all but invincible. All selfishness and self-centeredness is lost and one becomes centered in reality and truth."

To make his point, Sensei had one of the new students stand in front of him and push against him. The man was about six foot four and 220 pounds. He put his hands up to Sensei's hands and pushed, but Kuhara Sensei didn't move. Then the big guy really leaned into Sensei, but still there was no movement, no matter how hard he strained. Sensei had each of the new students try to move him, including me. None of us was successful.

Kuhara Sensei continued his lesson, "Aikido is a form of martial arts that is solely protective in nature. It doesn't teach kicks, nor does it teach offensive strikes, per se. Basically it is a method of protection in which the person being attacked uses the attacker's force and momentum to help create the attacker's downfall. It does not teach force against force, so you will not need to learn how to hold off someone larger than yourself, as I've just done. But if you continue to practice, eventually you too will learn how to use ki to your advantage."

Sensei had us pair up to start practicing the physical techniques. He put each of his new students with a more experienced student. My partner had a similar build to mine and he was about my age, though he was a couple of inches taller and probably a few pounds heavier than I.

"Hey, I'm Billy," he said, as we walked to our practice area.

"I'm David," I greeted in return.

Sensei yelled across the room, "I want everyone practicing the first five basic techniques."

I wasn't sure what to expect. As with most martial arts, there are different styles, and aikido was no different. I was curious to see how close my style was to the one I was about to practice. It didn't take long for me to realize that they weren't exactly the same, but they were thankfully from the same family.

Billy asked me to throw the first practice punch, and he showed me the first technique. As I moved toward him with a right punch, Billy slowly stepped in and to the right, avoiding the punch, and at the same time blocking the punch with his right hand. Next, he changed hands, finishing the block with his left hand, which freed his right hand to catch my chin, sending me to the mat. I managed a grin as I pulled myself from the mat. He had done the move perfectly. Now it was my turn.

"Do it slowly so you can make sure you do it correctly," said

Billy, not aware of how experienced I was. "The speed will come later."

I had done the same technique hundreds of times, so when Billy moved toward me with a punch, I moved flawlessly through the technique, effortlessly throwing Billy to the mat.

"That was good," he said, glancing up from the mat with a surprised expression.

We did the first technique again with the same results before moving on to the next one. As Billy looked up at me from the mat after I'd thrown him for the third time, he said, "You've done this before, haven't you? Here I was treating you like a beginner, and you know this stuff better than I do."

I grinned broadly, saying, "I don't know about that, but yes, I have done this before."

During the next hour or so, Billy and I threw each other quite a bit. It felt great to be practicing again, and I was amazed at how fresh my skills were even though I hadn't practiced for over four months.

As I exited the parking lot that day, I felt ready to deal with whatever came my way, forgetting the fact that aikido would be helpful to me only in certain situations, depending on how I was attacked. About halfway home, however, this hidden truth emerged. A man in a red Camaro, going in the same direction as I was, swerved into my lane, almost hitting my car. To avoid a collision, I jerked the steering wheel to the left, which made me cross the yellow line. The man in the Camaro laughed and gave me the finger as he pulled back into his lane and drove off. A loud whistle sounded in front of me, drawing my attention back to the problem at hand. The oncoming traffic was barreling down on me, specifically a giant, red dump truck full of dirt. Swerving to the right and back into my own lane, I made a narrow escape.

I pulled over to the side of the road to gather myself. I was still shaking from the incident when I got home.

While I was getting out of my car, Granddad came to mind. I hadn't talked with him since the night I had received the threat. For some reason, I hadn't been able to catch him at home. I decided to pay him a visit.

Granddad wasn't home when I arrived, but he walked up as I was leaving.

"What have you been up to this week, Granddad? I've called and come by, but you haven't been around."

"I've been doing some fishing. I found this great spot, and it's only about a half hour from here. You'll have to come with me one day. How about you? What you been up to?" he asked, as we sat down in the two rockers on the front porch.

"I hardly know where to start." I paused, trying to find a beginning, and then said, "Well, you know the other night when y'all came over to eat. After you and Jenny left, I received a threatening phone call from one of Lynn's old boyfriends. He said that he would kill me if I kept seeing her. Since then, he's called a second time and has broken in and torn up my apartment. And somebody just tried to run me into a dump truck, but I don't know if it was him or not."

Granddad listened, but said nothing, so I continued, "It's been a pretty scary experience."

"Sounds like it," he replied.

"For the life of me," I said, "I can't figure out why this is happening. Everything was going so well, and then all of a sudden things got real crazy."

We sat in silence for a few moments, and then Granddad said, "Maybe things are still going well for you. You just can't see it."

"Right! How could getting killed be good for anybody?" I scoffed.

"You're not dead yet, are you?"

"No, but it doesn't feel like things are going my way."

"No, it probably doesn't, because you can't see the results. You can't see where your life is heading. You can't see what part this experience is playing in the overall scheme of things. Here, let me tell you a story I heard while I was in China. It's from the *Huai Nan Tzu,* an old Taoist wisdom book. I think it'll help you better understand what I'm saying."

Granddad's eyes came alive as they usually did when he was

telling one of his tales.

Once there was a farmer and his son. They worked their farm together and used their one horse to plow their fields.

One day, the horse ran away, and they couldn't find it. No matter how much they looked, the horse was not to be found. All of the farmer's friends said, "What bad luck, to lose your only horse. Now you and your son will have to pull the plow yourselves."

The farmer replied, "Good luck, bad luck, who knows?"

A few days later, the farmer awoke to the sound of horses outside his window. Once outside, he found that his horse had returned with five wild mares.

All of his friends told him how lucky he was, but the farmer still said, "Good luck, bad luck, who knows?"

The next day the farmer's son tried to break one of the wild horses, but he was bucked off. When he fell, he broke his leg.

All of the farmer's neighbors shook their heads, saying, "What terrible luck. Now, you'll have to work the farm alone."

The farmer had the same thing to say as before, "Good luck, bad luck, who knows?"

A war broke out two weeks later and all of the able-bodied young men had to go fight, but since the farmer's son had a broken leg, he was spared. The neighbors could not believe the farmer's good fortune, and they told him so.

Once again, the farmer just said, "Good luck, bad luck, who knows?"

"We never know where life is leading us," said Granddad, after he finished his story. "Our paths have many winding turns. Right now, what you are experiencing appears negative, but where will it lead? It may lead to positive results in the end.

"When I was in my first year of college, I broke my arm playing football. That was not good; in fact, it was very painful. Then I had to go to the doctor and have it set. That wasn't good, either, but the nurse that I met at the doctor's office was good. And she became my wife and your grandmother, and that was very good. So, was the broken arm good or bad?"

"I see what you mean, but my situation is different. I could die. I just can't see much good coming from that."

"And there may not be any good to come from it, but 'Good luck, bad luck, who knows?' We don't know what lies on the other side of any experience. Death may not even be a tragic experience. It may be like walking from one room to another. In fact, it may be a wonderful experience. Who knows?"

"Do you think that's how it will be?"

"I don't think anyone really knows what will happen to us after we die, but my gut says it will be okay. So I just trust, and I no longer waste my time trying to answer unanswerable questions. Life and death are mysteries. God uses them to teach us. They are not to be understood, but experienced. Life finds our weaknesses and then brings us the lessons we need to make us stronger. It keeps at us until we learn, and then it moves us to a new level of lessons. We are always moving toward openness and balance, and that movement will probably continue even after we leave this life."

When I heard the word balance, my mind flashed back to the words of my new aikido teacher. It did feel as though life was constantly throwing lessons my way, placing teachers in my path at every turn.

Granddad continued, "Our struggle to feel good and to stay in control of our lives is the very thing that creates our suffering. If we didn't resist so much, most of our so-called negative experiences would not hurt half as bad, if at all. We think that events create the suffering, when actually that's not true. Our resistance is what usually creates our tension, fear, anger, and ill health.

"Until we learn to open up to life and let it take us on our journey… Until we trust our guts to lead us on our paths, we are just anxious creatures driven by fear and a desire for safety and security. Until we learn how to die in each moment and come to terms with our own fear of death, failure, and the unknown, we can never really live.

"We die many deaths every day, and each one is life's way of teaching us. We fail at this, we fail at that, we lose this game, we lose that relationship, and we lose our health. Life is teaching us all along that loss is all right, that death is okay, because with each death comes new life."

Granddad's eyes shimmered as he spoke, reminding me of fireworks on a dark summer night. His face was aglow. He spoke like the prophets of old, his message pouring forth from regions unknown, as if he could not hold it in, as if there was a fire within which would consume him if he didn't release it.

"Granddad, do you remember the other night when Jenny was so upset about Alex's friend dying and she didn't know what to say to the little girl's mother? Why didn't you share any of this with her? You didn't say a word. Why didn't you help her?"

It seemed wrong and uncaring to me that he hadn't helped Jenny when she was suffering so. He had kept the truth from her. He had kept it to himself.

"It was not a good time to speak," Granddad said in answer to my question. "My head wanted to tell her, but my inner self knew that silence was the best path."

"But you could have helped her so much."

"Maybe, maybe not. Maybe she was not in a good place to listen; maybe she was not ready to hear the truth at that moment. Or maybe she needed to wrestle with things herself first.

"What happens if someone helps a butterfly out of its cocoon?"

"I don't know. What does that have to do with you helping Jenny?" I asked.

"It has everything to do with it. If someone helps a butterfly break free, the butterfly loses the opportunity to build up strength in its wings. When it comes time to fly, it can't; its wings are not strong enough. Sometimes, we have to let people struggle so they can build up their strength. Otherwise, like the butterfly, they will be too weak to fly.

"Problems are the universe's way of building us up, of making us stronger. They are the universe's way of letting us know we have something else to learn."

"When you look at it that way," I replied, "problems almost seem like something we should welcome, rather than something to avoid."

"And so they are," said Granddad. "Life is a process of waking up to reality. Problems tell us that we are missing something and that we need to wake up. Every time we run into a challenge and learn to deal with it, it is no longer a problem for us. We can add it to the list of things we know how to handle."

I pondered Granddad's words and then said, "So, it's not really good to help people with their problems. They're better off solving their own problems, so that they can become stronger."

Granddad replied, "It depends on the situation. You have to listen within, to that still, small voice, to know what to do. Sometimes, it is more loving to help someone, because they need that kind of support. At other times, it might be better to let them solve their own problems. Only your gut knows what is best to do in each instance."

Granddad didn't really tell me how to solve my problem, but talking with him did help me feel better.

*   *   *

I didn't see much of Granddad over the next couple weeks, nor did I hear anymore from the person who had threatened me. Lynn and I talked about the threat now and then, but as time went by, it became less of a focus. I did, however, experience another dream.

It began with my walking through the woods listening to the

crunch of fallen leaves beneath my feet. Every so often, I would hear someone yell, "Timber," and soon after the yell, there would be a loud crash. There was something in the sound of the man's voice that was disturbing to me, but I couldn't figure out what it was. Not sure whether to go toward the noise or to run from it, I approached carefully.

Before long, a man with an ax appeared in front of me. He was large, like a lumberjack, but he was dressed more like a businessman. I hid behind a pine tree to watch him. He had black hair and wore dress pants, a dress shirt, and a tie. At first, his face was turned away, but then he turned toward me. It was the same man who had been watching me in front of the church, the same man who was in my third dream. It was Brian. I tried to run, but my legs wouldn't move.

Then our eyes met. He sneered at my paralysis. I tried to scream, but no sound came. I put both hands on my right leg and picked it up, moving it one step. Then I grabbed my left leg, moving it the same way. His laughter rang through the woods as he reveled in my agony. Again, I moved my right leg and then my left, struggling with each step, sweating profusely, thinking that I was going to die. Brian walked towards me. Again, I tried to scream without success. Just when he was about to touch me, the dream changed, and it was Lynn touching me instead of Brian. And as soon as she touched me, she took off running. I tried to follow her, but my legs still wouldn't work. Then I began to feel dizzy and out of sorts. I could barely keep my balance. I pursued her the best I could, but she was running way too fast for my lead-filled legs to catch her. In no time, she was virtually out of sight, and then she was gone. The more I strained to follow her, the dizzier my head became, until finally, I just gave up all together.

Soon afterwards, Granddad and his companions appeared.

Granddad handed me the book of light, saying, "Still struggling, are you?" Then he rejoined his comrades. Rather than disappear at this point as they had in previous dreams, they sat down to watch me as I read the words from the pages of light.

There is a constant flow
    of universal energy
and an energy door
    within you.

Whenever you hold on,
        tense up,
    and resist in any way,
        the door closes,
            cutting off the flow.

When you relax,
    let go, and trust,
        the door opens,
    letting in a constant flow
        of pure energy.

When life feels painful
and your energy is depleted,
it has little to do
with what is happening around you.

The problem is within;
you are closing up
and cutting yourself off from the Flow.

Beware of judgment
of self and others.
Nothing creates closure faster
than judgment.

Remember,
judgment creates judgment
and acceptance creates acceptance.

One opens the flow;
the other closes it off.

Love and accept others.

Allow them to be who they are.

Trust the universe
and the process of each individual.

Listen within
for what and
what not to do.

And seek,
not so much to do,
but to be.

Your doing may affect the actions of
others,

But it is your being that touches
their very souls.

7 Growth Pains

One might have thought that working with troubled kids, being in a new relationship, and having a maniac threatening my life would have been enough for me to deal with, but evidently the universe didn't think so. So it sent me some additional lessons in the form of Mrs. Tyson who, as I said, was one of my co-workers at Fair Hope.

Our problem began when Mrs. Tyson heard one of the girls at school call me "David." I was standing beside the water fountain waiting to get a drink when Nicole approached and asked, "David, is it okay for me to go talk with my social worker?"

"Sure, Nicole, go right ahead," I replied. No sooner were the words out of my mouth than Mrs. Tyson swooped toward us like a hawk to the kill.

"What do you mean calling Mr. Harper by his familiar name, young lady?" she asked with anger and resentment in her voice.

"He told us we could. He doesn't mind," Nicole replied.

"Well, I don't care," snarled Mrs. Tyson. "I don't want to hear it again."

"It really is okay," I said to Mrs. Tyson. "Recently, I've told all of the students they can call me David."

"Well, you can tell them to stop." Her eyebrows furrowed as she spoke.

I was taken off guard by her audacity. Who did she think she was, telling me what I could or couldn't do?

Since I didn't submit to her wishes, Mrs. Tyson decided to bring Christine into the argument during our next staff meeting.

"Mrs. Banks," said Mrs. Tyson, virtually spitting out each word, "Mr. Harper has been allowing the students to call him 'David,' and he has continued to do so, even after I told him that such a practice was not appropriate."

"Yes, usually the students do call teachers by their surnames rather than by their first names," replied Christine in a soft confident voice.

Mrs. Tyson gave me a smart-aleck, "I told you so" look, the kind of look that makes you want to knock the expression right off the giver's face. I could feel my heart beginning to beat faster and my face turning red with anger, but then Christine continued.

"But it's not my place to tell Mr. Harper what to allow his students to call him. He's a grown man, so if he wants them to call him 'David,' that's his business, not mine."

"Yes it is," Mrs. Tyson sneered between gritted teeth. Her scarce lips were drawn tightly against her hollow cheeks. "You're the coordinator of this school. If we start letting these children have freedoms such as this, they will lose respect for us and take over."

"Mrs. Tyson, I'm not sure I agree with you on that point," Christine said crisply, "but that isn't the issue." Then she turned to me, "David, are you having a problem with disrespect because of this?"

"No, I'm not. Ironically, the opposite is proving true. The kids seem to respect me more since I've allowed them to call me by my first name."

That was pretty much the end of the argument, but not the end of our conflict. After that, Mrs. Tyson seized every opportunity to attack anything that I did. Up until then, I had thought that she was just an unhappy person, but as the days passed, I began to realize that Mrs. Tyson might be mentally ill. She seemed paranoid to me. If I was nice to her, such as giving her a compliment about her hair or dress, she questioned my motives. If I reacted to her onslaught of nastiness with anger, then she saw that as an act of war and came on even stronger.

She ruled her class with fear and dealt with everyone as if they were an enemy. The students hated her. How she had come to be a teacher at a mental health facility was beyond my comprehension.

The next weekend, I spoke with Granddad about the situation. We talked while he was watering some newly planted azaleas.

He said, "This woman must really be suffering within to be creating this much pain around her."

I hadn't even considered her suffering until he brought it up. I had just thought of her as mean, unfair, and vengeful. Granddad always seemed to see things from such a unique perspective; I could rarely tell what he might say from one moment to the next.

"Rather than resist her, feel compassion for her brokenness and love her," he said, pulling the hose behind him as he moved.

"Be real, Granddad," I replied, walking behind him. "You haven't met this woman. That would be like loving a rattlesnake. She put the 'm' in mean."

"Do you want your relationship with her to improve or worsen?" he asked.

"I want her to stay away from me, and me from her. That's what I want. Mom always said, 'If you can't get along with someone, then stay away from them.'"

"Good advice when you can follow it. But can you?"

"Somewhat, but you're right; I still have to deal with her every so often. But Granddad, you don't understand. This woman is something else. The other day one of the kids tried to apologize to her for making her angry, and she wouldn't even accept the girl's apology. She just turned her head, didn't even speak to the student, and walked off. The girl who was trying to apologize is a pretty good kid who doesn't get into trouble like some of the other kids do, but she has gotten on Mrs. Tyson's bad side, and now she is paying for it. Just like I am."

"Okay," said Granddad, "let's say that this woman is as unhealthy as you think she is. You still have to work with her, don't you?"

"And how do you propose I do that?" I asked.

"First, try to understand her, and then choose to love her. Look past her behavior into her pain. Think about when you've been hurting and how your pain has sometimes led you to act like a jerk. And don't tell me that you've never been a jerk. We all have. Look inside, and find some empathy and compassion."

My mind filled with examples of my being nasty to people, including all the times I had yelled at a person when I was really angry at someone else.

Granddad went to the faucet, turned the water off and continued, "Pain often makes us lash out, even when we know better... We all are doing the best we can," he said.

"She's not doing the best she can," I responded immediately. "She couldn't be."

"How do you know?" Granddad replied, as we strolled to the steps to sit down. "What if she was abused as a child? Many are you know. What if her mother and father were cold and unloving towards her? What if she is living in a bad situation at home?"

"But we don't know that any of those are true," I said.

"But we do know that she is hurting."

"Yeah, that's probably true," I replied. "She probably is hurting."

The longer we talked the more my view of Mrs. Tyson evolved. She really was a sad case. She was miserable, and it must be wretched to live day by day with a constantly miserable person – in her case, herself.

"I see your point," I said. "Focusing on her pain helps me to see her differently."

"And it may help you respond differently, as well," he said. "When you can quit reacting to her as a threat or an adversary, your relationship with her will change. It has to, because she can't fight you if you don't fight back."

After pondering his words, I said, "But... if I don't watch her, she will nail me. She's quite articulate and verbally skilled, not to mention one hell of a manipulator."

"Okay, well then, use what you've been learning about staying aware. Listen to your gut and step back when you need to, but still send her love and compassion."

"What exactly do you mean by 'send her love?'"

"Wish her well; hope that she becomes healthier. Be friendly, but not overly friendly. Don't react and take things she does personally. Remember, it is her pain attacking you, not her."

For the next few weeks, I put Granddad's plan into action. I didn't expect immediate results, which was a good thing, because there weren't any. After a while, however, some changes did occur. Mrs. Tyson's attacks on me began to lessen, and she even seemed to become more cordial. It made me wonder if the problem had actually been mine rather than hers in the first place. Then I realized that she was still treating others as badly as ever, so at least some of the problem had been hers. I had to admit, however, that part of the problem had been my fault. Otherwise my changes in behavior could not have had such a dramatic impact on our relationship.

My life began to feel relatively calm. There was less tension between Mrs. Tyson and me. I hadn't heard anything from my would-be assailant for almost a month. And Lynn and I were closer than ever. Life was feeling pretty good. I even began to feel safe again, safe enough to go for walks and sit on the porch, two things which I hadn't done for over a month. I began to wonder if the danger was over, and I was cautiously hopeful that it was.

In light of my evaporating fear, I decided to invite Lynn over for a Sunday afternoon of guitar playing on the front steps of my apartment building. Lynn was getting better and better on the guitar. She had even started learning how to play the harmonica and the guitar together as she had seen me do at the party.

As I sat on my balcony waiting for Lynn to arrive, I was keenly aware of the beauty around me. It was a gorgeous October day; most of the leaves had already changed. Splashes of red, orange, and gold were everywhere. The sun was shining brightly from a cloudless sky, and there was a slight breeze blowing in from the west.

Fall was my favorite time of the year, not too hot and not too cold; it was just right. It was sweater weather, not cold enough for a coat, but usually a little too chilly for shirt sleeves. It was that time of year when the heat of the summer was replaced by a welcomed coolness. I loved to feel the chill of the fall air against my skin. It was like a wake-up call to my being. The coolness against my face helped me feel more alert. It also seemed to raise my energy. Cool weather made me feel more alive.

Fall was usually a peaceful time for me. It was a time for gathering myself together after the heat and activity of the summer. It was a time of contemplation, as well as a time of preparation for the coming winter. It was a time of change, of harvest, of death and dying. Yet in the midst of the change and dying, there were signs of promise and hope. The turning of the leaves was such a sign.

As I waited for Lynn, I thought about my fear of death, as well as my desire to hang on to life. Maybe death was not something to scorn, as I had always thought. Maybe it was beautiful, as natural as the changing of the leaves.

When Lynn finally drove up, I hurried down to meet her.

"Hi," I said, giving her a kiss.

"Sorry it took me so long; I just couldn't seem to get everything done this morning. It's been one big rush since I got up."

"That's okay," I replied. "I've just been sitting here enjoying the day."

"I wish I had time to do that."

"Yeah, it's nice. I wish I had more time to do it, myself. Here, let me get that for you," I said, as she reached in the backseat of her car for her guitar case.

"Thanks," said Lynn. "Speaking of free time, my parents are going to be coming through town on the way to the beach, and they're looking forward to meeting you. I've been telling them all about you for over a month now. You want to meet them?"

I had learned along the way that when a girl wanted you to meet her parents, the relationship was becoming serious in her eyes. I liked that, because our relationship felt serious to me, too.

"Yeah, I'd like to meet them. Just let me know when."

"They'll be here two weeks from yesterday. Can you come for supper?"

"That'd be good."

"Okay," she replied, apparently pleased.

While we were sitting on the steps actually doing more talking than guitar playing, Lucy, the little dog from next door, joined us. I was reminded of when Lucy and I had first met. It was one of the first days after I'd moved in. I had gone downstairs to sit on the front porch to relax with a bag of cookies and a glass of milk. I hadn't been sitting for more than five minutes when up walked Lucy, a little brown and white dog, who appeared to be a mixture of beagle and collie. She sat down right in front of me, offering me her paw. After we shook hands, she stood up and began shuffling her feet, wagging her tail excitedly. Evidently, she had been given treats for shaking hands before, and she was thinking that her handshake would buy her a cookie. At first, I was hesitant to give her one, but then I did.

Well, here was Lucy coming for another visit and more oatmeal cookies. So I ran upstairs to get her some. She was waiting at the foot of the steps for me when I returned. When she saw the bag of cookies, she went directly into begging mode.

Lucy was a smart dog. Since our first meeting, she had learned to bark when I said, "Speak," and to lie down when I said, "Go to bed." She already knew how to shake hands, and she was quite skilled in the art of catching cookies and popcorn in her mouth when pieces were tossed her way.

I always enjoyed Lucy's visits, and I tolerated the talks I had with her owner, Mrs. Abernathy, when she came looking for Lucy. Every street has a Mrs. Abernathy. She could tell you a little bit about everyone on the street and a lot about most of them. She knew who was dating whom, who had recently broken off relationships, and who was pregnant, as well as any other juicy bits of knowledge or trivia. She liked to compare the people who lived in certain houses or apartments with the people who had lived there in the past. Her memory was amazing.

On this particular Sunday, Mrs. Abernathy joined us almost as soon as Lucy did.

"Here you are, out of the fence again, Lucy," she said as she walked up, still dressed in her flowered pajamas and a pink robe, even though it was one in the afternoon.

"You're a bad dog," she said to Lucy.

Lucy didn't pay Mrs. Abernathy any attention. She was focused on the cookie bag, like a guru on a mantra. As I watched her, I envied her ability to focus. Concentration like that would be helpful during meditation. Oh, well... maybe one day, I thought to myself.

Then Mrs. Abernathy turned her attention to us.

"I haven't seen y'all for a while. Where you been?" she asked. Without waiting for a reply, she went on to say, "I heard someone broke into your apartment. Those damn treasure hunters! When are they going to realize that there aren't any jewels left in that building."

Lynn and I glanced at each other with perplexed, questioning looks.

"Oh yes," Mrs. Abernathy nodded knowingly. "Every few years someone shows up, breaks into every apartment in your building. They search and search, never finding a thing, but they have to look for themselves."

"When I first moved in," I replied, "I was told something about some jewels in this building. Do you know more about that?"

"Sure do," she said. "Your apartment was just the first one they broke into this time. The other upstairs apartment and one of the main floor apartments were broken into the night before last... You mean you don't know the story of the jewels?"

I could see that she was pleased that we didn't know. She sat down on a step below where Lynn and I were sitting and began her tale. Though I wanted to hear what she had to say, I hoped it wouldn't go on forever.

"You don't know the history of this building, do you?" she asked.

"No, except I heard that once upon a time an old millionaire lived here," I replied.

"This hasn't always been an apartment building," she said. "It's only been converted into apartments for about twenty years now.

"Anyway, this eccentric man named Pruitt lived here. He was a real oddball. He lived in this big old house all by himself. He was a very wealthy man, and it was said that in his earlier years he had been quite a playboy. Anyway, he was in the jewelry business, and it was rumored that he had stores all over the U.S.

"In his last years he was said to have large numbers of valuable jewels in his house. Or at least, that's what the papers said after his death. They had interviewed someone who had quoted Mr. Pruitt as saying, 'It would be pointless to own beautiful jewels if I can't enjoy them everyday.'"

I caught Lynn's eye and winked. Mrs. Abernathy's words spilled out in a rush, as though she feared interruption if she slowed down.

"When he died, he left all of his estate to his cousin. She was his closest relative as well as one of his best friends. When the media printed the story about the jewels possibly still being in the house, she refuted it. She said that Mr. Pruitt had asked her to take the jewels to the vault at his bank. The media still played with the story, however, and kept everyone wondering if there were still more jewels in the house.

"Finally, the cousin became so fed up with all the hype that she told a reporter, 'There are *no* jewels in that house. If anyone can find any jewels in there, they can have 'em!'

"'Do you mean that?' questioned the reporter. 'Can I quote you?'

"'Yes, anything to get you off my back,' she replied. 'Now, leave me alone.'

"You can just imagine what happened then. Every other day someone was breaking in to look for the jewels. They tore the place apart piece by piece. That went on for five or six months. Eventually, the building began to look pretty rough inside, and rather than selling it as a house, it was converted into apartments."

"That's one heck of a story," replied Lynn.

"That's not all of it," Mrs. Abernathy said. "About three years after the building had been converted into apartments, one of the tenants found some jewels in the upstairs apartment next to yours.

"Due to all of the stir, your building has had a lot of tenant turnover. In fact, I know of a few people who moved from one apartment to another looking for jewels. Heck, I think one man lived in every one of the apartments for a little while. And then there are the treasure hunters who break in and tear up the apartments, which drives some of the tenants away."

"So people don't really believe that all of the jewels were found, and they keep looking for more?" asked Lynn.

"They refuse to believe it. Their greed blinds them. Every few years, a new group of treasure hunters appears. One day everyone will realize that there just aren't any jewels left in that old building."

As Mrs. Abernathy was finishing her sentence, the strangest thing happened. I heard Lynn's voice in my head. I looked at her and our eyes met. Somehow, I knew what she was thinking, "So, Brian was not the one who messed up David's apartment; it was one of the treasure hunters."

Then she said, "Brian didn't do it; one of the treasure hunters broke into your apartment."

"You're right," I replied, but my mind was elsewhere, trying to figure out how I had heard Lynn's thoughts in my head.

"What are y'all talking about?" asked Mrs. Abernathy, her gossiper's curiosity piqued.

"Oh, nothing really," I said, pulling myself back to the moment to give Mrs. Abernathy the quick version. "One of Lynn's old boyfriends is jealous of me, and when my apartment was ransacked, we thought he might have done it."

"Oh," said Mrs. Abernathy, seeming to ponder my reply.

I was surprised that she let such a juicy-sounding story go by without making more of an inquiry. I shifted the conversation back to the jewels.

"But what about the jewels, Mrs. Abernathy? Why don't you think there could be anymore?"

"It's just not likely. I think that girl found the last of 'em, and now she's probably living it up in the Bahamas or somewhere like that."

"I wish I'd found them," said Lynn with a gleam in her eye. "I know I'd be living it up. I'd quit my job, and I'd travel for the rest of my life. I'd buy a new car and just about anything else I wanted."

"What would you do, if you had found those jewels?" Lynn asked, directing her question to me.

"I'm not sure," I replied. "How 'bout you, Mrs. Abernathy, what would you do if you'd found them?"

"I really don't know. I'm an old woman. My house is paid for, and I don't need much. I guess I'd sell most of 'em and put some of the money in the bank for a rainy day, and then give the rest to my kids."

"I'd probably sell 'em, too," I said. "Then I'd put the money in the bank and live off the interest. I'd keep teaching as long as I enjoyed it, but it'd be nice to know that I didn't have to work if I didn't want to."

"You wouldn't travel?" asked Lynn, with a disturbed look on her face.

I realized my mistake, and quickly said, "I would, if that's what my partner wanted to do."

Her face relaxed at my reply.

Mrs. Abernathy filled us in on the rest of the neighborhood news, and we played a couple of songs for her on our guitars. While we were playing, a large, furry gray cat walked up and started pawing at Mrs. Abernathy's leg.

As we finished the song, Mrs. Abernathy said, "Look at this cat. He's telling me that it's time for him to eat. Bagley," she said to the cat, "you're the bossiest thing… always trying to tell me what to do. You come and paw at me to let you outside; then fifteen seconds later you beat on the door to come right back in. I think you just like having power over me, like I'm your servant or something. You don't think I have anything else to do but take care of you."

"He's a pretty cat," said Lynn.

"Thank you. Yes, he is a pretty cat, but don't let him hear you say it. He already thinks he's the king of the house," she replied. "Well, I guess I better get these animals home and get 'em some food before this dog eats up all your cookies and this cat claws through my pajamas."

Mrs. Abernathy headed home with Lucy and Bagley. Lynn

and I went for a walk.

In the midst of all the hoopla about dogs, cats, jewels, and millionaires, I completely forgot about hearing Lynn's voice in my head. Then while we were walking, it happened again. We had just turned the corner from one street to the next when, as before, I could hear her thoughts.

She was thinking, "I wouldn't have most of these houses, but that yellow one is nice."

Almost immediately after the words entered my mind, Lynn spoke aloud a similar version of what I had heard, "I don't like many of these houses, but that yellow one right there is kind of nice. What do you think about it, David?"

I was so shocked that I couldn't answer.

"What do you think about it?" she repeated.

"Oh, I... It's nice," I said, stumbling over my words.

In the past, I had had experiences in which I knew what someone was going to say because of the circumstances, their body language, or what they had previously been saying, but this was different. I had actually heard Lynn's thoughts in my head.

Then it happened again. In my mind, I knew that she was going to ask, "Do you like picket fences?" and within seconds, that was exactly what she asked.

I couldn't help but grin.

"What's so funny?" she asked. "All I asked was, 'Do you like picket fences?'"

"Oh, nothing. Yes, I do like picket fences," I replied.

"What's going on?" she asked. "You're acting kind of weird."

"I was just in another world. I'm back now."

"Good, so which of these houses do you like?... You still have that silly grin on your face. What's going on?"

I couldn't decide whether I should tell her what was happening or not, but I had to tell her something or stop grinning.

Finally, I said, "I knew what you were thinking. I knew what you were going to say before you said it."

"Oh sure. Really, what's so funny? Do I have something on my face or in my hair? What is it?" she asked, as she felt around for foreign objects.

"No, it's nothing like that."

"Well, what is it?"

"I told you, I knew what you were going to say before you said it."

"You mean like knowing the time without looking at a clock. Now you can read my mind?"

"Not all of the time, just when there is a lull in the conversation."

"You mean, right now you know what I'm thinking?"

I tried to see if I knew, but I didn't.

"No, I don't know. I can't make it happen. It just happens on its own."

"You are the strangest guy I've ever dated," she said. "I don't think I like you being able to read my mind."

"I think it's neat, myself," I replied, grinning.

"How would you feel if I could read your mind and knew everything you were thinking? Think of all the things that I might learn that you would rather I didn't know. It's an invasion of privacy."

"You're right," I replied, "but it's not as though I'm trying to do it. It just happens."

"Well, make it stop."

"I don't know if I can."

"Try!" she said.

"Well, it hasn't happened since we've been talking about it," I replied.

"Good, because I don't like it," said Lynn. "I don't understand you, sometimes. And sometimes, you scare me."

"I don't mean to."

"But you know these things you're doing aren't normal, don't you?"

"But they could be," I said. "Remember what your minister said about a new reality? Maybe this is part of it."

"Maybe," she said, sounding unconvinced.

"Anyway, I thought you wanted to be different. I thought you wanted something other than the norm – the monotonous nine to five work week."

She didn't reply. The rest of the walk, I continued to have glimpses into Lynn's thoughts, but I didn't tell her about them anymore, and each time I had to fight back a smile to keep her from becoming suspicious.

By the time we got back to my apartment, she seemed to have forgotten all about the mind reading. She never mentioned it again, and neither did I. The rest of the evening went well, except that when Lynn tried to leave, her car wouldn't start. I fiddled with the engine, trying to get it started, but I couldn't, so I drove her home.

During the drive back to my place, I reflected on my day. It had been a wild one, what with the story about the millionaire and his jewels and finding out that Brian probably hadn't broken into my apartment after all, topped off by having experiences of spontaneous mind reading. What a day, I thought, as I turned onto my street. Little did I know that the adventures of the day were far from over. In fact, they had barely begun.

I parked across the street from my building, exiting my car. As I walked across the street, I heard: "It's about time you got back! I've been waiting for your ass!"

It was Brian. The sound of his angry voice sent me into a panic; I could feel my heart pound inside my chest. He was sitting on the front steps of my building. He held a bottle of beer in his left hand, and in his right what looked like a crowbar or a pipe. As he stood up, he placed his beer on the steps.

"You should have listened to my warning, you little shit. Now I'm gonna have to teach you a lesson. I'm fix'in to beat the hell outta you."

He began to move slowly in my direction, rhythmically hitting the crowbar into his left hand as he walked. His deep-set eyes stared at me. Brian was big. He was at least six-four.

I thought about getting back into my car and trying to get away, but there wasn't time. I considered running. Instead, I moved out into the middle of the street, trying to reason with him.

"Come on, now," I said. "We don't need to do this. No one is worth killing somebody over."

As he came closer, I detected the stench of stale beer on his breath.

"I'm not going to kill you, but when I get through with you, you'll wish you were dead," Brian replied, swinging the crowbar at my head.

I jumped back, throwing my arms up over my head as the crowbar sped past my face. I was surprised that he swung so soon. I'd thought he would talk awhile before attacking. I tried to gather myself together, but there was little time. The bar came slashing back toward me from the opposite direction. I twisted to my left, but the bar caught me across my right shoulder, sending a sharp pain down my arm all the way to my fingertips. I moved away as quickly as I could.

"Gotcha!" he said, laughing maniacally.

While Brian relished his success, I backed further away, testing my shoulder and arm to see if they were still able to function. Nothing seemed to be broken. I was in pain, but it could have been worse; it could have been my head.

I was not used to someone having the advantage of a crowbar during an attack. In aikido we had practiced against knives, and though approaching an attacker with a crowbar might be similar, there were some big differences. The length of a crowbar gave an attacker a tremendous advantage. I was going to have to do some quick improvising. I couldn't withstand many more blows like that first one.

I realized everything had happened so fast that I had reacted totally out of fear, not using any of my aikido skills. I was thankful for the few moments I had to gather myself. Suddenly, Brian lunged toward me again, swinging down toward my head with the crowbar. I dove down to the left under the speeding bar, rolling on my injured shoulder and popping back up to my feet as I had done so many times in practice. There were no soft mats to fall on this time, however; I had only the rough hard pavement to break my fall.

Quickly balancing myself, I prepared for his next assault. It came immediately in the form of a backhand swipe of the bar toward my chest. Again, I rolled out of the way, but this time, he was on me before I could regain my balance. I felt the bar come down hard against my right thigh. The pain was immeasurable. Then Brian swung another downwards blow, which I barely avoided.

"I'm going to beat the living hell out of you," he said, laughing as I dragged myself away.

He slowly walked toward me, raised the bar overhead and swung a powerful blow. Due to my leg injury and limited movement, I was forced to do what I had been taught and what I should have done from the beginning. Rather than trying to get away, I moved into him. When his arm came down, I caught it with my left hand and almost simultaneously caught him under the chin with the heel of my right hand. The combination of his momentum and my twisting to my left was enough to send him flying head over heels onto the road with a heavy thud.

He lay there a second or two before slowly getting up. I thought again about running, but with my hurt leg, it was not feasible.

"Now, I *am* going to kill you, you little bastard! I'm gonna crush your damn head with this bar," he yelled as he moved toward me, the bar hanging at his side. I backed away until he attacked. This time, when he came at me, I moved to my left, grabbing his right wrist as I went. I put the palm of my left hand against the back of his right arm near his shoulder. His momentum and the pressure I exerted landed him squarely face down on the road. He cried out in pain. Blood from his nose and mouth spilled out onto the pavement. I pinned his shoulder and arm to the pavement with my knee, and I wrenched the crowbar from his hand.

I looked around for help. A man and woman were standing on a nearby porch. I asked them to call the police. Brian struggled a bit at first, but he finally just lay there quietly.

When the police arrived, they put Brian into the back of the patrol car, and I managed to sit down on the steps of my building. My hands were trembling uncontrollably and my body was aching, but I didn't seem to be seriously injured. I felt thankful it was over, and that I was reasonably okay. I was mighty grateful for my aikido training, too. Without it, I was sure I would be dead.

8 Humility and Worth

A week and a half after the incident with Brian, I had my sixth big dream. It came the night before I was to meet Lynn's parents.

Once again, I found myself at a party. I was sitting on a sofa talking with an extremely seductive woman. Her dark hair hung in soft curls from the top of her head down to her creamy white shoulders. She wore dangling diamond earrings that swayed and sparkled every time she turned her head. Her low-cut white gown outlined the sensuous curves of her body, partially exposing rounded supple breasts. There was something wild, even devilish about her, yet something pure and angelic, as well. She was a wonderful, yet strange, mixture of opposites.

While she and I talked, her husband played darts on the other side of the room. He glanced our way every so often, but he didn't say anything.

Suddenly, something whizzed past my ear and stuck in the wall behind me. When I looked up, the woman's husband was preparing to throw a second dart my way. I jumped to my feet and took off down the hall. The second dart whizzed past my right ear. The third barely missed my left shoulder.

I stopped to pull the third dart from the wall, and then it was my turn to do the chasing. I threw the dart his way but I missed, and then he was after me again. Figuring that my luck was soon to run out and knowing that I had my Superman suit on under my clothes, I ducked into the bathroom, locking the door behind me.

I quickly undressed. Then I opened the door and jumped out with my hands on my hips and my chest bulging, just as I had watched Superman do so many times before.

But I was not Superman, and there was not a Superman suit on under my clothes, just regular old Fruit of the Loom underwear. So there I stood in white briefs and a T-shirt. And instead of a man with darts waiting for me, there was Granddad with his two companions in white, all three of them laughing. Granddad shook his head from side to side in apparent disbelief, and then he handed me the large shining golden book. Instantly, the three men disappeared. I opened the book and read:

Realize
  that
    in the eyes of eternity,
  you cannot increase
    or decrease your worth.

Your worth is constant.

Nothing you do,
  good or bad,
    can change that.

Humble yourself,
or humbled you will be.

Pride
is extra
and totally unnecessary.

Besides,
success
is not all it's cracked up to be.

It's greatly overrated.

It gives you a little buzz,
then it sends you off seeking more.

Think about it.

Accept failure
and success
as equals.

Both are part of you.
Both are part of your path;
each your teacher.

Each special in its own way.
Both lead you toward the Oneness.

Your goals and your agendas
　　deafen your ears
　　　to the still, small voice.

They blind your eyes
　　so that you can't see
　　　the path before you.

The best way to find something
　　is not to seek it.

Notify your mind of what you want,
　　open to it happening,
　　　then let it go!

And remember,

It's not your task
to teach others
unless you are led to do so from within.

Teaching
is the task of the universe.

Your purpose is to be you –
nothing more, nothing less.

But if by chance
you teach by being a healthy you,
that's
wonderful;
the universe
has used you as a lesson.

Granddad had a good belly laugh when I told him about my Superman dream.

"You *have* been pretty self-assured of late," he said between chuckles. "A bit too self-assured it appears. Huh, Superman?"

Though I had been feeling somewhat invincible since handling my situation with Brian, I definitely wasn't feeling that way when it came time to meet Lynn's parents. I wanted to make a good impression, and I wasn't really sure how to go about doing it. My anxiety level was high. Lynn's parents were planning to stay two nights with her, one on their way to Florida and another on their way back home. I was to join them for dinner both times.

The first meal went rather well, as far as I could tell. The weather was exceptional, so we cooked out at Lynn's apartment complex. Its excellent facilities included two gas grills. While our steaks cooked, we relaxed in lounge chairs beside the pool, sipped wine, and talked.

Lynn's parents were an attractive couple. Her father was a tall, distinguished, well-built man with graying hair and a well-trimmed beard. Her mother looked a lot like Lynn. She was short and petite, had blond hair, blue eyes, and a beautiful smile.

At first, our conversation centered around the subject of retirement and how pleasurable it could be if you prepared well while you were young. Lynn's father was really enjoying his retirement. He played golf nearly every day and he spent much of the rest of his time reading money magazines and studying the stock market.

Mrs. Whitmire's life had not changed much since her husband's retirement. She still worked out at the gym at least three times each week, played bridge one day a week, and remained active in civic organizations and clubs. Retirement had brought one nice change, however. Since retiring, they had purchased a beach house, which they visited often. She said that she loved the beach and hoped to live there one day.

We also talked about my family. I told them about my father dying and about my mother raising my brother, my sister, and me by working a part-time job and with the help of Social Security.

Mrs. Whitmire said, "Your mother must be a strong woman."

I laughed and said, "You don't know the half of it." I went on to tell her stories of my mother fixing the plumbing, as well as our car, because we didn't have the money to pay professionals.

Things were rolling along fine until the subject of employment came up. I guess I should have seen the problem coming, but I didn't. Lynn's father had a great attachment to wealth and did not see teaching as a viable profession. He said, "Teaching might not be so bad, if you made any money doing it."

Lynn tried to defend me and my profession, but it didn't

seem to help much. Her mother changed the subject and the atmosphere became pleasant again. When it was all said and done, Lynn and I felt my first dinner with her parents went fairly well.

The next morning, Mr. and Mrs. Whitmire left for the beach, and Lynn and I celebrated our apparent success by going out for breakfast. We even started talking about getting married and where we might go on our honeymoon. The rest of the week I floated with the clouds. I was as happy as I could be, and I sang or hummed Christmas songs all week long: "Dashing through the snow in a one horse open sleigh. O'er the fields we go, laughing all the way, Ha, Ha, Ha... I'm dreaming of a white Christmas, just like the ones I used to know... Silver bells, silver bells. It's Christmas time in the city. Ring-a-ling, hear them ring. Soon it will be Christmas Day..."

A lot can change in a week. So it was with that week. While Lynn's parents vacationed on the sunny beaches of Florida, the temperature dropped in our area. The newsman predicted an early winter. Just as Lynn's parents returned, the cold set in, but the weather outside was not the only chill we felt. The entire second evening with Lynn's parents was a frosty experience. Neither Mr. nor Mrs. Whitmire would make eye contact with me, and the conversation was strained.

I tried to slough it off as nothing and not take their behavior personally. Maybe they had had a big fuss during their trip, I rationalized.

At the close of the evening, Lynn walked me to my car. She apologized for "her parent's weirdness" and said that she didn't have any idea why they had behaved as they did. We kissed good night, and I went home.

The next morning it was apparent that something more had happened. When I stopped by to pick up Lynn for church, her parents were gone, but the chill remained. On the way to church, she had little to say and she seemed to be avoiding eye contact with me, much as her parents had done the previous evening. After church, she declined my invitation to lunch, saying that she wasn't feeling well. When I asked if there was anything I could do, she said she needed some time alone.

I called to check on her that evening, but I only reached her answering machine. After four or five attempts to reach her by phone, I decided to go by and check on her. She wasn't home.

The next day, there was a message from Lynn on my machine, "David, give me a call when you get home. We need to talk."

My stomach turned upside down as I listened to the message. Something was wrong! Seriously wrong!

I called immediately, "Lynn, what's up?"

"You probably need to come over," she said. "Can you come now?"

"Yeah, but what is it?"

"I really don't want to talk about it over the phone."

"Just tell me," I said.

"No, I don't want to talk about it until you get here."

"Just tell me."

"Okay," she said. "I don't think we should see each other anymore."

I was speechless. How had we backpedaled from talking about marriage and honeymoons a few days before to not seeing each other?

"I'll be right over," I finally stammered.

On the way to Lynn's, I sorted through every possible cause for her change of mind, but I could not get a grasp on what had happened.

Lynn greeted me at the door, but she was cool.

"I don't understand," I began, going straight to the heart of the matter. "How did we move from getting married to not seeing each other?"

"We're just not right for each other, David."

"How is that?"

"I don't know. It's a lot of things."

"Like what?... Name one."

"Well,... I don't feel needed by you."

"You don't feel needed. Well, you are. I wouldn't be here if you weren't."

"But you don't n-e-e-e-d me," she said. "You have your life all worked out. I'm just an ornament in the background. I need to feel n-e-e-e-ded."

There was a long silence. I felt confused. I had thought she wanted a confident, strong man who could take care of her. Where was all this coming from, I asked myself. I felt frustrated beyond belief.

She continued, "It's not your fault. You're a great guy. Any woman would be lucky to have you."

"Any woman, but you," I retorted.

"It just would never work," she replied, "I hope we can still be friends."

She wasn't giving any concrete reason. All kinds of thoughts went through my mind, but none of them made any sense. My whole life was falling apart, and she was giving me the dreaded line, "I hope we can still be friends."

"I do need you, Lynn," was all I could think to say. "Your love and support are part of my strength. Don't you see?"

"But I need to be more than that," she replied, "I need a man that I can help—one who really *needs* me."

"I do *need* you," I repeated.

I left Lynn's that day, bewildered and hurt. I agonized that evening and the whole next day, searching for answers. Lynn's reasoning made no sense. There had to be something else. Maybe she was just going through some pre-commitment jitters and would soon come to her senses.

I wanted to call her, but I decided to wait a couple of days before doing so. Maybe she just needed some space.

In the meantime, life had to go on. I still had to work and keep functioning.

Nothing felt okay. One day everything was more than perfect and the next everything had fallen apart. My life was way out of balance. My stomach was a wreck, and eating was out of the question. When evenings rolled around, sleep came only after hours of lying awake. The mornings were just as difficult. After having little sleep, pulling myself from bed took tremendous effort. I just wanted to pull the covers over my head, but I managed somehow to get up and go to school.

Since I wear my emotions on my face, my students immediately knew something was wrong. They sympathetically questioned me. They were patient and sensitive beyond belief, considering they were emotionally conflicted teenagers. Their sympathy attested to the fact that I was growing. I had absorbed some of Granddad's wisdom and had moved closer to the center. My growth had shown in class, and the kids were responding in kind.

However, when I was not able to snap out of my depression, they began to lose it. My class started to feel like a war zone again. Although my students had come a long way in the two and a half months since school began, they were still disturbed teenagers in a treatment center. They were not strong enough to work independently for long. They needed structure and encouragement. And since their leader was regressing, they were following close behind.

After school on Friday, I gave Lynn a call, but there was no answer. Disappointed, I tried to reach her again and again. Finally, on my fifth try, she answered.

"Hello, David," she said.

I didn't know what to say. Hours of pondering had led me to the conclusion that her parents must have had something to do with her change of attitude, but I didn't know how to broach the subject.

"Can I come over, so we can talk some more?" I said finally.

"No. I don't know if that would be a good idea. We probably need to make this a clean break and not drag it out. Talking more will just make it harder on both of us."

A raging anger rose within me. "I thought you said you wanted to be friends," I snapped. "Whatever happened to that idea? Did it get thrown out with the idea of getting married?"

She didn't reply.

I continued, "Did your parents have something to do with you changing your mind about us?"

"They had nothing to do with it," she snapped back, venom in her voice. "I make my own decisions. They liked you. We're just not right for each other. Can't you face that?"

"But you didn't come to that conclusion until after you talked with them, did you?"

"They care about me, and they're just looking out for my happiness. They know what's best for me. They know what I want and what I need. You won't ever be able to provide for my kids and me like my father has provided for his family."

So money was the culprit. That hurt. My heart felt as though it had just been ripped from my chest. I couldn't have felt any worse.

9 The Emptying Process

Over the next couple of weeks I wanted to call Lynn, but I refrained. It probably wouldn't have done any good anyway, and begging was not my style. Depression and sadness took over. My troubles with eating and sleeping, as well as my challenges at school, became worse. So many questions raced through my mind. Where was God when I needed Him? How could He give me Lynn and then take her away so suddenly?

Then I thought about the unusual things that had happened while I was with Lynn: the time-telling without a clock and the mind reading. Surely, God didn't want to tease me by letting me experience such extraordinary talents, and then just take those talents away. But they happened only with Lynn, and she was gone.

As a child, I had coped with hurt or disappointment by crawling under the bed or hiding in the backyard with my dog or my stuffed animals. Those tendencies had carried over into my adult life. I spent the first three weeks after the breakup as a recluse, only leaving my apartment when it was absolutely necessary – only to go to work. The hurt was simply too painful, and the embarrassment I felt was almost as bad. Meditation was the only thing that felt at all pleasing to me and at times, even it was a struggle.

Thanksgiving came and went with my not feeling thankful for anything. My loss enveloped my mind, not allowing me to focus on anything else, including all of the many blessings that were present in my life.

Christmas approached, but I hardly noticed. December had always been one of my favorite months of the year, but this time it turned into a period of isolation, loneliness, and extreme sadness.

I didn't tell anyone about the breakup until a couple of weeks before school was to end for Christmas holidays. It was a Friday afternoon, and Christine, my boss, had stopped me in the hall as I was leaving. She looked pale and washed out.

"I need to speak with you," she said, "but first, are you okay? You haven't seemed yourself the last few weeks."

Part of me wanted to tell her, but another part wanted to run and hide.

"Are you okay?" she asked again.

"Lynn and I broke up," I said softly.

"I'm sorry to hear that. Is there anything I can do?"

"I don't think so; it will just take time. But thanks for asking. You don't look so good yourself. How about you? Are you okay?"

She didn't answer at first, and then she said, "You have enough to deal with." She appeared even more disturbed than before.

"Christine, something is wrong. I can tell."

After a long pause, she said, "I have lung cancer."

I grimaced at the words. "What?… When did you find out?"

"Wednesday. I haven't been feeling well for a while now, which is not like me, so I finally went to the doctor, which I never do. They did a battery of tests and found that I have a tumor in my left lung."

"But you don't smoke," I replied.

"No, I don't. They're not sure what caused it. I don't guess it really matters."

"Can it be treated?"

"Yes, but the tumor is fairly large, and its location is such that they can't remove it. The doctor has set up a plan of a combination of chemotherapy and radiation treatments."

"Well, at least that sounds hopeful."

"They've been very honest with me. They're not expecting a

cure, but they're hoping to buy me some time, possibly a couple of years. They are hopeful because the scans didn't show any metastasis, but they said that doesn't necessarily mean there isn't any."

"I'm shocked."

"I guess that's where I am, too," she replied.

I put my arm around her, and she leaned against me slightly for a moment before pulling away. As she backed away, I noticed a tear rolling down her cheek.

"I can't do this here," she said, wiping her eyes. "I don't need to be crying."

My mind raced back to my pastoral care classes in seminary in an attempt to find the right words to say. Then I remembered that there weren't any so called *right* words. Christine was suffering, and all I could do was *be* with her the best I could.

"Crying helps let the pain out," I said finally.

"I know," she replied. "That's all I've done for the last two days."

We went to her office to talk, and the longer we talked, the smaller my own problem became. When we had finished – nearly two hours later, Christine said she felt better having gotten it all out and she thanked me for listening.

My concern for Christine had shifted my mind from my own problem. Feeling less depressed, I decided to stop by Granddad's on the way home.

Granddad answered the door with a cup of marshmallow-topped hot chocolate in his hand. Steam rose from the cup, and the smell of chocolate filled the air. It was cold and rainy outside, so when he offered me some, I heartily accepted.

We sat on the sofa in front of his fireplace, and as we sipped our chocolate, I told him about Lynn and her parents, as well as about Christine. Granddad listened quietly, yet intently, absorbing every word I said. He didn't speak; he just listened.

"Granddad, what do you think I need to do?"

"About what?"

"About any of it. What are you thinking?"

"I'm not thinking much of anything, David. Mostly, I'm

listening. You're dealing with some tough stuff. I'm not sure that you can do anything to change any of it, but you might be able to change how you're looking at things."

"What do you mean?"

"Well, you can't make Lynn love you, and you can't cure your boss's cancer, but you can do something about how you deal with your feelings about both situations."

"Like what?"

"Well, first of all, you have to decide what you are going to do with your sadness. If you fight it, it will just get worse. I recommend you step back and ask yourself, 'If I have to be depressed, then where do I want to spend my depression? Would it feel better to sit on the porch and look at the trees? Or go to the park?' It's okay to feel the sadness and pain, but don't wallow in it isolated in your apartment. Step out and do something pleasing in the midst of feeling the pain. Accept the sadness, and be easy on yourself. And remember, magical things happen when you want to be where you are."

"That might be true," I said. "But right now, I'd be lying if I said that I wanted to be where I am. Lynn and I were talking marriage. I just can't understand why she did this."

"Are you looking for an explanation?"

"I don't know. I just want her back."

"I know you do."

"But why would this happen, Granddad? I mean, after the prayer and all. Why would God give me Lynn as an answer to my prayer, and then take her away? I just don't understand."

"I'm not sure that understanding is really what you're seeking, but if you think an explanation will help, I'll give you one."

"Okay. Yeah, it might help some if I better understood why this happened," I replied.

As he had done so many times before, Granddad picked up one of his drawing pads to draw me a picture. It was a drawing of two half circles facing each other.

He said, "Each of these semi-circles represents a person. We can call them David and Lynn or Julie and Don. It really doesn't matter, because this happens to everybody.

"Notice that I didn't draw full circles, because most of us are not whole; we are still filling out our circles. Like these two people, most of us search high and low for our perfect match, not realizing that the universe has other plans for us, at least in the beginning. The universe uses our sexual drives and our need for companionship to motivate us in certain directions, so that we can learn the lessons we need to learn.

"Usually, we are drawn to people to whom we are sexually attracted or to people who enjoy some of the same interests we do. Then later, this passionate encounter between apparent soul mates becomes a struggle with someone that we thought we knew, but didn't. Often times, one of the two decides to leave and continue on his or her search for Mr. or Mrs. Right. The one who is left feels betrayed and bewildered, until he or she finds another apparent soul mate. Then, the same thing happens all over again. Again and again, our half circles get up enough courage to try love one more time, not realizing that their need for companionship and sexual gratification is the universe's way of spurring them along on their journey toward wholeness.

"All of your relationships have taught you something, David. Each one has helped you become more complete. Each one has helped your circle grow. Eventually, you will become a whole circle. Lynn came into your life to help you in that process, but not necessarily to be your life-long partner."

"But what about my prayer?" I asked.

"What about it?" he replied.

"Why would God give me what I asked for and then take it away?"

"I'm not sure that's what's happened," said Granddad.

"What do you mean?"

"That's *your* interpretation of what happened. We don't know for sure that your interpretation is right."

"But how else can you see it?" I asked.

"Well, prayer may not be so much about asking for things as it is about listening. To me, prayer is more about us getting on *God's* wavelength rather than us trying to get God on *our* wavelength. Maybe you got what you asked for because, for that moment, you were tuned-in to what you needed; you were on God's wavelength. Perhaps now, you're more tuned-in to your desires, instead of the reality of what you need."

"I think I see what you're saying Granddad," I said, "but still, I want somebody to love and somebody to love me. I want a relationship that will last. I need somebody I can count on, somebody I can trust, and I thought Lynn was the one."

"Who's to say she's not? But it seems apparent that she's not what you need right now. And whether she's the right one for you or not is irrelevant. To have the kind of lasting relationship you're looking for, you're going to have to get yourself together first. As you become more centered, the rules of attraction will begin to shift, because you'll have less need to attract opposites into your life. As you become healthier and your circle fuller, the potential for finding the kind of partner you seek will increase. After you learn to accept everyone and everything, then you'll begin to attract your likeness. That's just how the system works.

"How can you attract a healthy person to your life if you're not healthy yourself? What would you have to offer them?"

What Granddad was saying seemed to make perfect sense. I wondered why I hadn't realized it before.

Then Granddad drew two complete circles on the pad.

"When two complete circles meet," he said, "neither of them has to depend on the other to make him happy. Both are free from selfishness and consequently, are able to share their fullness with one another. Instead of one being the giver and one the receiver, both are able to give and receive freely. But to have this, you must first take time to work on yourself. So, you take care of your part of the process, and then trust the universe to take care of its part; it'll send you the right partner."

As I left Granddad's that day, he encouraged me not to be in such a hurry. "Don't try to rush it," he said. "Life is lived one second at a time. Learn to be okay in each moment. Don't try to rush through the sadness. Just feel what you're feeling. Accept and trust."

I did just as Granddad had suggested. I paid particular

attention to where I chose to spend my experience of sadness and grief over losing Lynn. His advice proved to be sound. I spent a lot of time rocking on the balcony of my apartment and going for long walks in the cool, December air. The weather was perfect, sixty to sixty-five degrees in the day, dropping into the mid-forties in the evening. Finding that I had some control over my feelings and my environment even when I was depressed, coupled with the great weather, gave me a real boost. My energy began to increase, and then it became easier to be objective, to step back and take a more realistic look at my life. The loneliness and depression that I'd been feeling began to feel more manageable.

By the last day of school before the Christmas holidays, I was feeling the need to get out some. I didn't really want to socialize, so I decided to wander around one of the local malls to finish my Christmas shopping. Christmas was usually an enjoyable time of year for me. Since I always did most of my shopping in October, I was free to enjoy December and all of the festivities without having to fight the crowds or worry about what to buy in the midst of the holiday chaos.

I had presents for everyone on my list except Alex, and he would be easy to buy for. So instead of going right to the task at hand, I bought a butter pecan ice cream cone, and sat on a bench in the middle of the mall beside a large sparkling fountain.

"Dashing through the snow in a one horse open sleigh..." played in the background, as hundreds of shoppers rushed by with their treasures in hand. Some seemed cheerful, but many looked stressed, worn out, and frustrated.

There was a long line of children with parents waiting to see Santa. He was seated in the doorway of a large, red and white cardboard castle. One child was being more than a handful for his mother, and she slapped him on the leg. Somehow that didn't seem right. The more closely I looked, the more stress and frustration I detected. Why were so many people trudging through the mall feeling completely miserable? It didn't make sense. This was supposed to be a joyous time of year.

A fussy little blond-haired boy and his mother came to the bench where I was sitting. The mother was an attractive, slender woman with her auburn hair coming loose from the bun on the back of her head. I imagined how she might have looked earlier, her hair pulled tight to her head and her make-up just so. But now her hair was coming undone and she looked worn out.

As the lady turned to sit down, a large woman overloaded with Christmas packages bumped against her, knocking her sideways into the bench. "Ouugh!" she said. Then to the woman she yelled, "Watch where you're going!"

The other woman never even turned her head, but kept a steady course, clearing a path as she went.

"Are you okay?" I asked.

"Yeah, I'm okay," she replied. A tear rolled down her cheek. Then she turned to her son and said, "Come on, Jimmy. Mama can't take it anymore. Let's go home."

"We wish you a Merry Christmas. We wish you a Merry Christmas. We wish you a Merry Christmas and a Happy New Year…" played mockingly in the background as the woman and her son left the mall.

I finished the last bite of my ice cream and began to make my way through the crowd, people bumping and pushing all around me. I heard an occasional "Excuse me," but more often I heard the negative remarks of the person who had been bumped.

After a few minutes, I strolled into the toy section of one of the larger stores where I noticed crowds of people gathered around two televisions. They were watching players competing in video games. Strange beeps, whistles, and other noises came from the T.V.'s, as well as some upbeat and funky sounding music. I joined one of the throngs, watching for a while.

As I looked on, I became more and more amazed, first at the skill of the players, and then at the graphics and the intricacies of the game, and finally, at how similar one of the games was to real life. The game consisted of a cartoon-like creature who scampered along gathering silver coins while trying to avoid the many obstacles springing up along its path. There were flying insects that shot pointed stars at the creature and spiked rodents that tried to ram him as he sped along.

The little creature rushed around gathering its treasures, much as the people in the mall were gathering presents. I thought, "We are all just video game characters in the cosmic game of life. We run around frantically doing this and that, thinking that the things we are doing will ease our pain and make us happy, but I'm not sure there is any more meaning to our rush and struggle than to the struggle of this video game creature."

Suddenly, my attention was drawn back to the T.V. screen. A bumble bee-looking creature came from nowhere, zapping the little coin collector as he tried to dash by. Silver coins went bouncing everywhere.

"Shit," cried the boy, as he maneuvered the controls, trying to gather up what he could of the disappearing coins.

The tension in the boy's neck and hands pointed to the stress he was putting on himself because of the game. His hands trembled as he guided the speeding creature away from another possible disaster. The boy was just another example of the tension and stress that seemed to be everywhere in the mall, everywhere in the world. Everyone was striving for something, striving for what they thought would make them happy and avoiding discomfort at every turn.

I had seen enough. I realized that I had been doing the same thing to myself over Lynn. Life had to be more than a struggle to get people to love me. It had to be more than striving for success and falling apart every time things didn't go my way.

I worked my way through the aisles of toys, looking for a present for Alex. I saw a little boy about Alex's age playing with a remote control dump truck that emptied its load with the push of a button. There was no doubt in my mind; it was the perfect gift for Alex. As I paid the cashier, the thought crossed my mind that it would be nice if everyone had a dumping button like the dump truck I was purchasing. Whenever our lives got too filled up with emotional baggage, we could just push the button to get rid of it all.

Taking my package from the counter, I worked my way through the crowd until I found a place to sit and sort through the myriad thoughts flashing through my mind. For the next half hour, I observed and reflected. My life was no different from the lives of the shoppers around me. Somehow, we had all lost our way. We had become robots driven by competition, desire, tradition, and habit. How had we gotten to such a state of existence that even our celebrations had become more struggle than joy? There had to be a better way.

The next morning, I awoke early to sit beside my bed in meditation for over an hour. Granddad had said, "Just go into the silence as often and as long as you can. The results will take care of themselves. Don't judge your meditation; just do it."

During my Christmas vacation, I spent a lot of time in meditation. Each day, I spent at least a couple of hours in the silence, and then I would go for a long run. I also took time to write in my journal.

When school resumed in January, I was beginning to feel strong again. The time off had given me a much needed opportunity to gather myself, and I had taken it. It was not as easy, however, when the holidays were over and I had to factor in the time restraints of having a full-time job. Finally, I decided to stop by Granddad's for some more advice. I felt ready to do whatever it took; I was not going to live a life of stress and struggle any longer.

I went straight to the point, "Granddad, I need your help. Over the holidays, I got a taste of heaven, and now that school is back in session, I'm losing it. There's just too much to do and not enough time to get it all done. I don't know what to do about it. I can't seem to get my life in order. I just can't seem to keep myself focused."

"Are you meditating regularly?"

"I was, but I haven't been able to over the last few days. I just don't have time."

"There's always time. You just need to do some soul searching and reexamine your priorities. Besides, you can't really afford not to meditate. Remember my story about Martin

Luther? Meditation is a time saver, not a time spender."

"Okay, let's say that I meditate every morning. Then there's another problem. When I get focused in the mornings, it doesn't last throughout the whole school day, and I am at loose ends before I get home to do my second meditation. What do I do about that?"

"Then take a time out. Or you could just meditate all day long."

"I'm serious, Granddad."

"I'm serious, too," he replied with a straight face. "I call it meditating my day."

"You're serious?"

"Certainly," he said with a laugh. "It's really quite simple. All it takes is a little faith, a bit of determination, and the genuine willingness to slow your life down. All you have to do is incorporate your breathing into everything you do, and then watch out for unawareness loops."

"I'm not following you."

"Okay, when you sit in the silence, you focus on one thing, and you let everything else come and go. Often times that one thing is your breath. Right?"

"Yeah."

"In meditating your day, you focus on your breath as part of your actions."

"So, if I'm doing something like washing the dishes, for example, I would be aware of my breathing as I washed," I replied.

"But you're not just aware of your breathing," said Granddad. "You're aware of the whole *now* moment. As you breathe, you breathe in the whole moment and all that is happening in that moment. You're aware of the air flowing in and out of your chest, and you're also aware of the warmth of the water, the softness of the suds, as well as the smooth texture of the dishes and the hardness of the silverware. If you really get into it, you start becoming one with everything you do and everything around you. It's a wonderful experience."

"That works?"

"It does for me. Your ability to focus is affected primarily by how open or closed you are. When you let yourself become a part of the present moment and experience and appreciate what you are doing, instead of resisting, striving for goals, or wishing you were somewhere else, then focusing becomes easy. Focusing is only a problem when you are torn and conflicted.

"Resistance creates negative thoughts, which in turn create negative feelings. Negative feelings tend to make us shut down and pull back. This closing up temporarily cuts off our universal energy supply. Sometimes our resistance also gets our adrenal glands to kick in, and once we are on an adrenalin rush, it becomes really difficult to gather ourselves together again. That's why addictions and compulsions are so debilitating. They grab us and get us going, and then they won't let us go."

"So, anytime I resist or want things to be different from the way they are," I said, "then I automatically make focusing more difficult?"

"That's right. The next time someone does you wrong or things don't go your way, notice what happens. If your boss gives you a disapproving look, step back and watch yourself. If you can feel what you're feeling without judging and resisting it, everything will be fine. But if you get lost in your feelings or try to push them down, your energy door begins to shut, and you lose your ability to stay in the moment."

"You're saying that anything I welcome and appreciate opens me up, and anything that creates discomfort, anxiety, or stress closes me up, distancing me from the source?"

"That's right," Granddad said. "If a pretty girl says 'Hi' to you, your door opens. If you spill coffee on your shirt, it closes. That's why forgiveness and love make you feel good. They open you up. And hate and fear feel bad, because they close you up. Once you start to close up and lose awareness and focus, things just get worse. You begin to lose your objectivity and your ability to step back, and then you move into what I call an unawareness loop."

"A what?"

"Let me get a pad and pen, and I'll show you. It will be

easier for you to understand if you can see it."

Granddad grabbed a notebook and a pen from a nearby shelf and began to draw what looked like an upside down tornado, the point of the tornado being at the top of the page with the larger circles at the bottom.

While he was drawing, he said, "Everyone experiences periods of unawareness. But people who go into the silence often, tend to stay aware for longer periods of time and have less trouble with unawareness loops.

"What we want to do is shorten our periods of unawareness and move into what I call an upward spiral." Then he pointed at the diagram, saying, "See how the loops become smaller as the spiral moves upward closer to the point? As we simplify our lives and take time to be still more often, our periods of unawareness begin to decrease, gradually becoming smaller like the circles at the top of the spiral. When we reach the pinnacle or total enlightenment, the loops disappear altogether and we become totally aware."

I was silent, trying to absorb it all.

"So, really," I said finally, "it all comes back to doing the things that help you stay balanced and open, like simplifying your life and doing your meditation."

"That's the long and the short of it," replied Granddad.

We talked a few more minutes. Then Granddad walked me out to my car.

"I'm going to try what you said," I told him, as I opened the door of my car. "I'll let you know in a week or two how it's working."

"I'm afraid you won't be able to do that, David. I'm not going to be around for a while. I'm going out of town in a couple of days and won't be back for a year to a year and a half, maybe longer."

"A year and a half!" I exclaimed in total shock.

"Or longer."

My heart sank. "Why?" I asked.

"Actually, for a few reasons. I've been waiting for this day, waiting for you to become totally committed to creating a new life for yourself. Now it's time for you to go solo.

"Parts of the journey you can take with others, but there are a few segments which you must travel alone. You've got all of the information you need. Now you just need to use it. And it sounds like that's where you're heading.

"Also, it's time for me to get back to the mountains. I need to go every now and then – to center myself. And it won't seem as long as it sounds; I'll be back before you know it. Besides, you have some interesting adventures ahead of you, and you won't be needing me around for a while."

"That's what you think," I replied.

"Remember, the universe and your gut are your primary teachers. I'm just an assistant," he said with a smile, and then his expression became serious. "David, there is one other thing I must tell you before you go. As you become more focused and begin to see things as they truly are, you will experience both ecstasy and darkness. At first, you will probably experience a feeling of great wonder and a happiness beyond what you've known, but then as you see more and more, the happiness will turn into a grief beyond all grief. When you get there, don't fight the pain. Accept it, and feel it. Once you open to it, it will pass right through you."

"What are you talking about, Granddad?"

"Just remember, don't fight the pain. There's not really anything else you…"

Movement in the yard next door distracted my attention from what Granddad was saying; a large black and white cat had caught something and was playing with it. On closer observation, I realized that it was a bird, so I ran toward the two of them yelling, hoping to frighten the cat away. The cat tried to grab its prey and run, but when I got close, it chose to scamper under some nearby bushes, leaving its prize behind.

The little robin was in terrible shape. She was barely alive when I reached her. She was a pitiful sight with a broken left wing and a broken left leg. Her tiny eyes looked dull and lifeless. It appeared that the life force was rushing from her body, and there wasn't anything I could do to stop it.

Granddad walked up beside me as I was examining the dying bird.

"That damn cat," I said under my breath.

"It's not the cat's fault," replied Granddad. "She's just doing what comes natural. She's a hunter."

"I don't care what she is. You want me to just walk off and let her finish what she started? It doesn't much matter, now, anyway. This bird doesn't have a chance. Look at it."

"What's your gut say to do?"

"To kill that damn cat."

"Are you sure that's your gut you're listening to?"

"No," I said, disgusted with the cat and myself. "But it's not fair. This bird didn't do anything to that cat."

Granddad put his arm around me and said, "Who knows what's fair and what's not." Then he sat down on the ground, picked up the bird, and cradled it to his chest like a baby.

"What are you doing?" I questioned.

He didn't reply. His eyes slowly closed, and it appeared that he was going to meditate right there in his neighbor's front yard. I looked around to see if anyone was watching.

The next thing that happened was nothing short of a miracle. The bird's eyes began to open and brighten, and then Granddad opened his hands and lifted the bird skyward. To my amazement, the robin spread her wings and flew away.

"Granddad!" I exclaimed in disbelief.

He didn't reply as he stood up beside me.

"You just healed that bird."

I'm not sure why it amazed me so, in light of all the other seemingly miraculous things he had done over the last half year, but it did. I stood there in delighted amazement.

"I can't get anything past you, can I?" Granddad replied, with a slight, unassuming chuckle.

"How did you do that?"

Without answering, Granddad turned to walk back toward his house.

I ran to catch him, grabbing him by the shoulder.

"How did you do that?" I repeated.

"It's just a matter of listening inside, emptying your mind, opening to the universal flow of energy, and giving from the overflow. You can do it, too. It just takes practice," he said. Then he walked up the steps to his porch.

"Wait a minute, Granddad. If you can heal people like that, why don't you do it all of the time? Think how many lives you could save."

"Healing is not the main issue here," he replied. "None of the masters went around healing anybody and everybody, now did they? They only healed when their guts led them to do so. Usually they used their healing skills as a tool to help people see the possibilities and to wake people up to their own potential.

"It's often better for people to go through their struggles and experience some pain and suffering. Such experiences build compassion, empathy, and humility and help them grow in ways that healing could not.

"But here you've got me explaining things again, don't you?" he said, chuckling. "That's enough talk for now. See you in a year or so." He opened the door to his house and started to enter.

"Hold on, Granddad. I don't think I understand. Now how do you know when to heal and when not to?"

"David, start answering your own questions. You know the answers," he replied, disappearing as his front door closed behind him.

Once again, Granddad's words set me to pondering.

10 Stepping Back

With Granddad no longer around to guide me, I had to learn to depend more on my gut and other resources. I spent much of my free time sitting in the silence beside my bed or in front of the fireplace watching the dancing flames. Being alone so much was a challenge at first, but after a while, the time alone became something I cherished.

I saw Jenny and Alex occasionally during this time, but they were the only human beings I saw other than the people at school and aikido. Jenny didn't approve of my being so reclusive, and she told me so. She called every week, saying, "I'm just making sure you're still alive." And I had to admit that even though I was staying to myself, it was nice to know that Jenny was there if I needed her.

Granddad's advice to meditate by being aware of my breathing throughout the day proved helpful, but not immediately. My old habits haunted me. I still wrestled with striving too hard, being in a hurry much of the time, not managing my time well, and closing up when adversity appeared. It took all of the determination I could muster, along with all that I had learned over the last year, to deal with my dysfunctional habits.

It wasn't until September of my second year in Birmingham, seven months after Granddad had left for the mountains, that I began to notice some truly significant changes occurring in me. I began to feel myself becoming more aware – aware of my body, my feelings, and all of life around me. Slowly, ever so slowly, a new, more peaceful me began to emerge.

The more I accepted life and myself and opened to the truth, the more realizations came my way. And the more aware I became, the simpler it was to continue along my path.

Those were some of the best months of my life. They weren't exciting. In fact, they were pretty low key and even boring at times, but wading through the loneliness and boredom was well worth it, because on the other side was a taste of heaven.

The frills and distractions of my life fell away and contentment started to become a part of me. Nothing seemed to bother me anymore. Not even Eric.

One day while I was teaching, little flashes of light kept flashing past me. They briefly flickered on a wall and then moved. I paused, trying to find the source.

There it was. Something shiny was dangling from Eric's ears. I walked toward him. I saw that Eric was wearing shards of mirror attached to his ears with paper clips. As he moved his head, the reflection from the mirrors bounced onto walls and other objects. It was a call for attention.

I smiled at him. "Eric, would you like to tell us about your invention?"

He shrugged and broke into a lop-sided smile. "It's just a little somethin' I thought up," he said. He shook his head vigorously, so that the reflections danced.

The class whooped and hollered. They loved the distraction, and they seemed genuinely impressed by Eric's strange device.

I walked closer to Eric's desk. As I approached, I noticed that he had a Penlite flashlight in his hand. "That's really quite inventive," I told him. "Stand up and show the class."

He hesitated, suddenly self-conscious. He asked, "You're not mad?"

I shook my head "no."

He stood and turned in a circle so everyone could see his creation as he shone the flashlight on the pieces of mirror. He sat as soon as he had completed his 360 degree turn. He looked at me as though for the first time and said, "Man, you ain't the same guy you used to be."

I smiled. "No, I'm not the same guy I used to be. I've learned a few things myself since coming here to Fair Hope. And I'm glad you've noticed the change."

"But you're an adult. You're not supposed to change."

"Eric, every day we live, we can learn and grow. You, as well as me." I put a hand on his shoulder. "I've got to get on with class. But I'd like to talk some more later if you want. Maybe after class. And then I can get a better look at your invention, too."

He nodded, turned off the flashlight and slowly reached up and removed the mirrors from his ear lobes.

Yes, life was much easier in those days, because I was more relaxed and not pushing so hard. I had let go of some of my need for control. Life just flowed, and I flowed with it.

However, toward the end of my second year of teaching, the happiness I'd been feeling began to fade. The change started one day, just a few weeks before school was to adjourn for the summer. I had just finished teaching a class on values clarification, my last class of the day, and I was on my way out of the building to go home when Christine stopped me.

She pulled me aside, "David, I'm resigning as coordinator of the school at the end of the school year."

"What?" I asked. "How come?"

"My cancer has spread. The doctor thought it was responding to the treatments, but my most recent scan shows metastasis to the liver. He said that I probably have less than six months to live, so I'm going to visit my sister in Florida and spend some of the time I have left at the beach with her."

"Can't they do anything?" I asked.

"No, I got a second opinion, and they pretty much agree. My body can't take much more radiation. And I'm not willing to go through any experimental chemotherapy just to buy a little more time."

"I don't know what to say," I replied.

"I don't quite know what to say myself. It just is what it is. And for whatever reason I don't feel afraid. I feel proud of my stamina through all of this, and appreciative of my medical care as well as the love and support of my friends and family."

Though Christine was a real inspiration with the way she was handling her situation, something about it was disturbing. As I listened to her, a feeling of hopelessness came over me. It was much like the feeling that I had had at five years old when my dad had died. Again, I felt that something was wrong. Something was *terribly* wrong.

Over the next few days the feeling became stronger, and my world began to grow extremely dark. Though Christine's impending death had been the catalyst for my depression, the problem went much deeper. Suddenly nothing made sense to me anymore, and I could feel the darkness closing in around me.

I had heard of such dark times when I was studying the desert fathers and some of the other mystics who had lived on the fringes of spiritual reality, but I had never known anyone who had experienced such a period of extreme darkness. I felt as if I were going to die. All of life as I had known it seemed without purpose. I couldn't make sense of any of it. I felt as if my world and all of its meaning had been stripped from me. The pain from such a loss of purpose and meaning was unbearable.

I had searched so long for meaning and purpose, and now I was realizing that there was none, or at least none that I could be sure of. All beliefs were just that, *beliefs!* People had nothing else to ward off the thoughts of nonexistence, so they turned to beliefs. There was nothing else to bet on, nothing else to help them make it through the hard times. But no one, not even one person knew for sure that his beliefs were true.

There were probably bits of truth in every belief, because each one had some grounding in reality. But all fell short in one way or another and all of a sudden, I knew why. All beliefs were made up of words and thoughts. They were just reflections of the nature of things, but just as a reflection in a mirror was not the same as the objects it reflected, a belief about reality was not reality itself.

I realized that my finite mind would probably never understand eternal reality. Depression swept over me.

I saw my life for what it was – a continuous effort to feel safe and secure, to avoid hell, to avoid pain, to be somebody, to have purpose, to count, and not for the short haul, but forever. I wanted to matter. I wanted eternal security, happiness, and purpose. Suddenly, I realized that nothing I could say, think, feel, or do could achieve that.

Those days were pure hell. Many mornings, I could hardly pull myself from my bed. I don't know what kept me going. I felt like a hollow machine, doing what I had been taught to do, going through the motions. There was no heart in my actions. The time I spent at school was awful, but the lonely evenings were even worse. At least at school, I would sometimes quit thinking and just do what had to be done. But at night there was nothing to distract me from my thoughts, nothing to ward off the emptiness and pain within me.

The end of the school year eventually came, but I felt no relief when summer began. I tried everything to get rid of the pain: exercising, walking in the park, buying myself presents, but nothing helped. Going into the silence helped a bit, but it didn't bring the peace and comfort that it once had.

Christine stayed on my mind a lot during those first few weeks of the summer. I felt sad for her, myself, and the school. She was certainly going to be missed.

Thoughts of her dying, mixed with the freedom of summer vacation, led me deeper within myself. My periods of meditation became longer, often approaching two hours at one sitting. The emptiness grew deeper and darker even in the silence, but there was something in the silence that made the emptiness bearable. It didn't take it away, but somehow it made it more tolerable. I couldn't quite figure out how the silence was helpful, so I finally quit trying. Every time I tried to make sense of it, the emptiness would take over, making the pain unbearable once again.

The more I fought the darkness, the more I seemed to hurt. Finally, one Saturday morning, while lying in a tub of hot water trying to feel something other than anguish and pain, I contemplated my choices. I saw no way out of my predicament. If life was no longer worth living, then why go on? I was not really suicidal, but I did consider suicide as an alternative and then concluded it was not a solution. Still, there was no fight left in me; the struggle was over. Life had beaten me. It had won. Tears rolled down my cheeks, dripping onto my already wet chest. I just wanted the pain to go away. I surrendered.

In the midst of these feelings of total emptiness, something amazing happened. I became keenly aware of the warmth of the water against my skin, the feel of the smooth porcelain beneath my body, the markings on the wood panels of the bathroom walls, the trees blowing outside my bathroom window, the dripping of the faucet. Then I realized the darkness was gone. In its place was the experience of the present moment – no thoughts, no feelings, just pure awareness of the reality around me. Granddad's words, "Don't fight the pain. Go through it," echoed back to me, and I grinned for the first time in weeks. Evidently, I had passed through.

A feeling of fullness moved into the void, into the emptiness that I had been feeling, and I saw the emptiness and the fullness in a new light. They weren't different; they were actually one and the same, two sides of one thing, two sides of reality, two sides of the Oneness.

Peaceful, happy thoughts and feelings came to my awareness, but somehow they were different from before. I had thought my feelings and thoughts were me, but now I saw them in a new way. They were both me and not me at the same time. They were like an extension of me. And just as the emptiness and the fullness were separate and one at the same time, so were my thoughts and myself, separate yet one. In fact, everything was that way. Everything was part of me, yet separate from me, all at once.

Some of the veils of illusion had been removed, and though I may not have been seeing reality as it truly was, I saw some of it more clearly. Though paradox surrounded my every thought and none of it really made sense, it didn't matter. I felt awake and totally alive.

As I dried off that morning, I knew that my life would never again be the same. It might continue somewhat as it had. I might even fall back into old ways for brief moments in time, but I sensed that because of what I had just experienced, things would always be different.

I began to spend a lot of time beside a small stream which ran through the center of a park not far from my apartment. The park was a beautiful touch of nature in the midst of the city. It was surrounded by tall pine trees, with magnolias, oaks, and maples interspersed throughout. It was just large enough to allow me to get away from city life for a while, and I took advantage of its offerings every chance I could.

I would sit beside the flowing water for hours, serenely watching it pass on its way over and around the rocks that protruded from the stream's soft sandy bottom. Watching the water, as well as listening to its rippling song, was a soothing balm to me.

Since I was feeling better and had so much free time, I started attending aikido classes three or four times a week, instead of just twice a week as before. I was planning to test for my black belt in the fall, and I needed to practice as much as I could to make sure that I was ready. Kuhara Sensei seemed pleased by my renewed intensity and dedication, as well as my progress. About the middle of July, he pulled me aside to talk.

"David," he said, "your physical techniques are excellent. You aren't going to have any problem at your fall testing. My intuition says it would be good for you to go ahead and start working on some advanced skills. We need to improve your inner focus and develop your use of ki. If you're willing, I want you to start practicing blindfolded some each class."

"Blindfolded!" I exclaimed.

"You don't have to; it's up to you. But for your development, that's what I recommend. Practicing blindfolded will make you pay closer attention to details and will eventually help you deal more effectively with even small distractions. It will help develop your sensitivity and encourage you to trust your intuition and your instincts, because without your eyes to guide you, you will be lost if you don't listen within."

The first of my blindfolded practices was a joke; my partner dominated me easily. I spent more time rolling on the mats than

I did standing up. The next few practices were no better, but Kuhara Sensei encouraged me to stay with it. Finally, after three or four weeks, things started to improve. I began to hear my inner voice more distinctly and respond to its leadings. My ability to defend myself improved. I was no longer always the one rolling on the mats. It was amazing to realize how much I could do without sight and to think that one day I might be able to protect myself without the benefit of my eyes.

I spent much of the summer meditating, practicing aikido, and running every other afternoon. With each day, I seemed to grow more in touch with myself. I was still somewhat isolated. I was still not dating or having much to do with people except at aikido. Then one day I had an experience, a forewarning of sorts, that signaled the end of that period of my life.

I was sitting beside the stream, listening to its rippling music, and I drifted within. Thoughts of Lynn, Granddad, my mother, and Christine danced in my mind. A great peaceful sadness filled me, and then an image appeared. It was an image of my sitting in meditation. As I watched myself, the image that was me seemed to lose its substance, becoming transparent. Within this clear shell, pictures began to form: images of my childhood, my friends, and many of the adventures we had shared.

As I watched, I began to see how each part of my life had been built upon the parts that had preceded it, each leading me along my path. The vision shifted from childhood, to adolescence, to college and seminary. There were images of my mother and father, Granddad and Christine, and Alex and Jenny. I saw how each one had played a part in my growth and I in theirs. All were part of the unending chain of my life and my development. As I watched the images, the chain continued until the present, but didn't venture into the future. I realized that though my growth had been immense, there was still more for me to learn.

All at once, the images ceased, replaced by a small crystal floating in the center of my being. I immediately recognized it as a symbol of my inner self. As I gazed at the crystal, it lost its substance, becoming a small, glowing orb. Then it began to expand, filling my stomach and chest with light. It grew larger and brighter, filling every part of me and expanding out beyond my bounds. I could no longer tell what was me and what was not me. All was one! I was the light and it was me. Then the vision began to fade, but the feeling of oneness remained, and a voice within said, "It is time. She is coming."

As I walked home that day, an air of anticipation enveloped me. But I was careful to keep myself balanced and not let the excitement take over. I had come too far to be enticed into the realms of excited unawareness for very long. I slowed my stride to focus on my breath, the air coming in, the air going out, aware of each step as I took it. A relaxed smile came to my face. I had come a long way. Walking up the steps of my apartment building, I wondered if anything would ever really shake me again.

When I opened the door to my apartment, it was again in a shambles. The "treasure hunters" as Mrs. Abernathy had called them, had returned, looking for jewels. Just as before, every piece of furniture had been pulled away from the walls, and all of my drawers, cabinets, and closets had been emptied. But this time, instead of feeling angry and annoyed, I just sat on the sofa, relaxed and at ease. Why not? Would becoming angry improve the situation?

"Whew, what a mess. But at least they didn't break much," I said aloud.

After a few moments, I began to straighten things, breathing slowly, still feeling the peace from the park flowing through me. I pushed the sofa in place across from the mantle, rearranged the tables and chairs, and placed the pictures back on the wall. It was a shame that one of the frames had been damaged, but it was repairable. I laid it aside, against the wall, and headed for the kitchen.

After dishes, clothes, and odds and ends were all back in place, I poured a glass of apple juice and headed out to the balcony to sit for a while. It was dusk, and the crickets were already singing. The lightning bugs were out as well. They had always fascinated me. Memories of catching them as a child flooded my mind.

As it grew darker, stars appeared in the clear sky. The night was intoxicating. I closed my eyes and listened to the crickets. Gradually, I drifted within. My mind was no longer full of the chaos and chatter of years before. Instead, the emptiness caressed me in its soothing, gentle manner. I had not a care in the world. I no longer needed to strive. I sat peacefully as a part of the universe around me. I smiled as my eyes gradually opened, letting in just a glimmer of light. I sat with my eyes half open, continuing to breathe in the sound of the crickets and the universal energy as it filled my body. Then I stretched and walked back inside to fix supper.

As I entered the kitchen, the blinking light on the answering machine caught my eye. I turned it on to hear, "David, this is Teresa Banks, Christine's sister. Christine's not doing well. Please give me a call at Christine's house as soon as you can."

I was surprised to hear that Christine was back in town. I called immediately.

"Hello."

"Yes, is Teresa there?"

"This is she."

"This is David Harper. You left a message on my machine about Christine."

"She has been asking for you. Could you come over?"

"Right now?"

"Yes, if you can. I don't think she has long."

"Sure, I'll be right there."

I was shocked. Christine was supposed to have had about six more months to live. It had barely been half that.

When I arrived at Christine's, Teresa answered the door. "Come in," she said.

As I stepped into the foyer, I noticed a young, dark-haired woman sitting across from an elderly couple in a room to the left. They looked my way, but said nothing.

Teresa offered, "That's my mother and father. They just arrived, and they're speaking with the hospice nurse about Christine's condition."

Teresa led me down a long hallway, past many shelves of antique vases. Christine was a collector. I had been to Christine's a couple of times before, and each time I had been amazed at all of the exquisite pieces she had gathered. In fact, her whole house was a work of art, from the Picasso prints on the wall down to her antique Victorian furniture.

The hallway darkened as we neared Christine's bedroom. Her room was dark too, except for a small lamp on a bedside table. As I stepped up to Christine's bed, I stopped in disbelief. Her face was severely emaciated. She looked as if she hadn't eaten for weeks. How could she have gone down so much since I last saw her?

"Christine," Teresa said, "David is here to see you."

She opened her eyes very wide, as if she had been startled or was disoriented and was trying to get her bearings. Christine didn't speak for a few moments. Her eyes had a glassy, unaware look about them.

"Hello, David… When did you get here?" she finally asked.

"Just a few minutes ago."

"I'm not doing too well. I can't keep my mind together."

"That's hard to deal with, I bet," I replied.

"My mind just comes and goes. It's the medicine. Where's Maggie? The nurse?"

"Oh… uh… I'll get her," said Teresa.

Christine's eyes drifted shut, and she was gone again. In just a few moments, the hospice nurse entered the room.

"Christine," the nurse said.

Again, Christine's eyes popped open. "I need some medicine for my stomach."

"Are you feeling sick?"

Christine nodded.

The nurse left the room, quickly returning with some pills and a cup of juice. She was so gentle as she helped Christine lift her head to take the medicine.

Christine grimaced as she tried to swallow the pills.

"Here, try another sip of juice," said the nurse. "Those pills are hard to swallow, aren't they?"

Teresa motioned to me to follow her into the hall, so I did.

"The cancer has been even more aggressive than they thought it would be," she explained.

"I'm sorry."

"Me, too."

"How long have y'all been back from the beach?"

"About two and a half weeks. Christine said she wanted to die at home."

The nurse came to the door, "She's asking for David."

When I returned to her bed, Christine looked a little more alert.

"I'm not doing well, David," she said again while reaching for my hand.

"I know."

"You have to do me a big favor."

"What is it, Christine?"

"I want you to do my funeral."

My mind reeled. I didn't know how to preach a funeral. I had skipped that class in seminary because I had no intention of ever being a pastor of a church, and I figured I would never have to do one. But what could I say? I couldn't say, "No."

"Okay," I said, trying to hide my reluctance.

"Maggie and I have talked about what kind of service I want. She can fill you in. You know, I drift in and out so."

I looked at the nurse. She was a confident young woman. In fact, her demeanor overflowed with confidence. A feeling of "it will be okay" came over me.

Christine and I talked a few more minutes before she drifted away again. Then Maggie and I went into the hall to talk, leaving Teresa with Christine.

"I will be glad to help you in any way I can," she said.

"Thanks, I'll need it. How long do you think she has?"

"She probably won't last long, now that she's talked with you. That seemed to be her last main concern. She has said her good-byes, but she didn't want just anyone handling her funeral."

"Christine said that you could fill me in on what she wanted in the service."

"She told me that she wanted a simple service and that she wanted you to do it. She didn't want anyone to preach a long sermon, using her death as an opportunity to manipulate people's minds. She thinks highly of you. She told me to tell you, 'Funerals are for the living, so say some comforting words, and then bury me.' She just wants something simple."

Christine died a week later. I saw her a few more times before she passed, but we never really got to talk much again. Each time, she seemed to have moved further and further away. It was a difficult time for me. Not since the death of my father had a death touched me so deeply.

Deciding what to say was a strange experience. Preparing words for any funeral probably would have been challenging, but having my first funeral be for someone I loved made it extremely difficult.

I didn't know where to begin. What should I say to people who have lost a loved one? Why did Christine have to die this way, and why right now? What is death? Is it the end or a new beginning? And how do life, death, and God fit together?

After hours of wrestling within, I was still at a loss for words. So at two in the morning, the morning of the funeral, with paper and pencil laid aside, I sat down beside my bed and let go of my task, closed my eyes, and let the silence wash over me. It wasn't long before the service began to take shape in my mind. An hour later, my eyes slowly opened. The service had more or less planned itself. I picked up my pencil and paper, writing it down.

"Now if the talk itself could be this easy," I said aloud to myself.

But the talk wasn't as easy, at least not at first. When I stepped behind the podium and looked out at all of the people, my stomach twisted into knots and a lump filled my throat. The church was almost full. There were probably over 150 people present. I scanned the audience for a friendly face. At first, my eyes met only the eyes of strangers, but then I saw some of the boys from the school in the back left of the sanctuary. Beside them sat Mr. Franklin and Mrs. Tyson. My body relaxed a little.

Scanning further, I saw Jenny and Alex in the back right of the church. Jenny had insisted on coming when she realized how nervous I was. "You're my brother," she had said. "Certainly I'm coming. You could use the support, couldn't you?" She was a special one, that Jenny.

I began the service with a prayer, and then I sat down while one of Christine's friends played "Paccabel's Canon" on the flute. The song had been one of Christine's favorites, and Christine's mother had insisted on the tune being played.

When it came my turn again, I stood up and said, "We are gathered here today to celebrate the life of Christine Banks." As the words passed my lips, I looked towards Christine's family. Some of them were crying, tears rolling down their cheeks. Others were fighting back the tears. One of Christine's cousins was crying uncontrollably. Small children sat close to their mothers, frightened by all of the emotions around them.

A tear slid down my cheek. I stood in silence for a moment. I glanced away from the family, hoping to pull myself together, wondering if I had made the right decision in agreeing to do the service. Though I was speechless, there was no panic within me. Underneath the chaos in my head, there remained a deep stillness. And then I saw Maggie, Christine's hospice nurse, sitting just behind the family. Her words came back to me, "Keep it simple, say some comforting words, and bury her."

My mouth opened. I listened to the words as I spoke. Throughout the talk, my eyes wandered back to the comforting gaze found in Maggie's eyes. I could feel her cheering me on.

I ended with: "Christine was a strong person – a good person. She saw the best in everyone, and she inspired all to become better. We all loved her. She was easy to love. We are grateful that she touched our lives – for every life she touched was made better by her contact. We will all miss her."

I stood in front of the church as people passed by giving me hugs, telling me how touched they were by my words. Mr. Franklin and the boys came by and said, "Hi." Jenny gave me a big hug and said, "That was beautiful. You did a great job."

The church emptied little by little until only the family, Maggie, and I remained. As we left the church, Maggie and I ended up together.

"Christine would have been pleased," said Maggie. "In fact, I have a feeling that she *is* pleased. You described her just as she was."

I didn't know what to say, so I just smiled and said, "Thanks."

"No, we thank you," she said, as we began to walk down the front steps of the church.

"No, I mean thanks for being so supportive while I was speaking. My eyes kept coming back to yours. I could tell you were with me and that you were listening. It helped."

"You're welcome then," she said. "Glad to be of help, but I wasn't the only one listening. That was one of the best funeral services I've ever attended, and as a hospice nurse, I've been to quite a few."

"It was an unusual experience," I said. "The words just kind of flowed out of me."

When we reached the parking area, we said, "Good-bye," and I walked toward my car. But as I went to open the door, I felt uneasy inside, as if I were leaving something. Also, I didn't really feel like going home.

"Maggie, hold on a minute," I called to her across the parking lot.

She was just opening the door to her car and she looked up. I trotted over to her.

"Somehow, it doesn't seem right to go straight home after a service like this."

"I was just thinking the same thing myself," she replied.

"Would you like to go get a cup of coffee?"

"I haven't eaten lunch yet," she said. "Would you mind going somewhere that I could get something to eat?"

"Now that you mention it, I haven't eaten either. I'm hungry, too. There's a little sandwich shop not far from here."

"I'll follow you," she said.

At the sandwich shop, I found myself nervous and tongue-tied as we sat down at an empty table.

"You said very little about death and heaven during your talk," said Maggie, once we were seated. "I was curious why you didn't venture into those topics more. Most ministers do."

I was surprised by her question, as well as her straightforwardness.

"I don't know," I stammered. "I don't think about those things much anymore."

"I'm interested though," she said. "Tell me what you do think."

"Well, I know we all die, and I don't think we will really find out what's next until we get there."

As she was pondering my answer, I turned the question back to her, "What do you think, Maggie?"

"I agree with you. We won't actually know what's on the other side until we get there," she replied. "But I've seen quite a bit in my work with the dying that encourages me to believe that there is something incredibly beautiful and comforting waiting for us after we die. I have often felt God's comforting arms around my patients and their families, as well as myself. I believe that we go from the arms of love here into the arms of love there. As a hospice nurse, I deal with death almost everyday, but you know, the more I experience it, the less afraid of it I become."

"How's that?"

"I think it's because of the beauty that it brings."

"Death?" I questioned.

"Yes, death. You should see the closeness and love that occur in some families as they take care of a dying loved one. I've seen it bring people together who have been angry with each other and haven't spoken for twenty years."

"That's such a positive way to look at it. But don't you get tired of the actual dying – of losing people that you've grown to love?"

"Sometimes, but most of the time it just makes me humble

and thankful. I feel privileged to be with people at such an intense and important time in their lives. And it's a wonderful reminder to me to stay focused on what's really important in life. Also, it's taught me how to trust."

"What do you mean?"

"I haven't gone to school and studied theology like you have. I've learned most of what I know just by living, and I've found that trust is the key. Since I don't know for sure what the truth is, and I haven't run into anyone that has convinced me that they know either, I've had to count on my trust to bring me through."

"Trust in God?" I asked.

"Yes. I believe that God loves us and that even though life doesn't seem fair sometimes and doesn't seem to make sense, it will one day. God knows my heart. So, I just do my best to trust and do what is put before me in the most loving way I can."

I felt drawn to this lady. She had great depth and was so natural. There was nothing put-on about her.

We talked for nearly two hours before Maggie glanced at her watch. Then, with a shocked look that turned into a grin, she said, "I've really got to go. I didn't realize it was so late. I've still got two patients to see today."

After I walked her to her car and was heading back to my own, I had a strange feeling that I was leaving something again. As I continued on, the feeling changed to an eeriness washing over me. I felt as though I were being watched. Turning around quickly, I spied a large dark-haired man getting into a maroon Firebird, and even though I didn't get a good look at the man, he reminded me of Brian.

It's probably nothing, I thought, as I got into my car and headed home. It had been more than a year since I had dealt with Brian. Surely, that was history.

11 Full Circles

It was three weeks after the funeral, and I was walking down Jenny's street on the way home after a long run. I was thinking about Maggie. I had truly enjoyed my time with her. She seemed spiritually minded and somewhat of a free thinker, two traits which greatly appealed to me. Being around her was a bit like being around Granddad – I just felt better in her presence. It's funny how some people can affect you that way.

As I approached Jenny's house, I noticed she was out front pulling weeds from her flower beds, so I stopped to talk for a few minutes.

"Hi, Jen."

"You been running?" she asked.

"Yeah," I replied, plopping myself down on the grass near her. "Is Alex around?"

"No, he's at a friend's house."

"Those impatiens are pretty," I said. "That's an unusual shade of pink; it's almost mauve."

"Yeah, they are kind of unusual." I watched her work in silence for a while, and then Jenny asked, "What's happening with you these days?"

"The same old thing for the most part."

"Have you seen that nurse anymore?"

I had told Jenny that Maggie and I had gone out for lunch after the funeral, and about our conversation.

"No," I replied, "but I've thought about her a lot."

"Why don't you give her a call?"

"I don't know. Besides, I don't know her number. I don't even know her last name."

"Call her at work."

"I hadn't thought of that, but… I don't know," I said shaking my head.

"Aw, go ahead. I can tell you want to. What's the worst thing that can happen?"

I shrugged.

"It's about time you found somebody, settled down, and had some kids. You would make a great father. Alex loves you to pieces."

I laughed at her. "Now, how did we get from my asking her out to my having kids?"

"Well, it seems like a natural progression, don't you think? You need a mate. You love kids. You love playing with Alex."

"That's different. Alex is yours. I'm not sure I want to have any of my own. Maybe if I could skip the diaper, sleepless years, and start off with 'em about Alex's age, that might be all right."

"But it doesn't work that way."

"I'll just keep playing with Alex, then."

"But you're missing out," said Jenny.

"Maybe so… Besides, I'm not sure that I really want to get involved with anyone. I've come to appreciate living by myself. Dating would bring a lot of changes."

"Not if you find the right woman."

"If I could have a woman who… if I could find one who comes at life kind of like I do. You know, one who is spiritual but still knows how to have fun, then that might work… but she'd have to be willing to spend some time alone, because I have to have my alone time."

On the way home, I decided that Jenny was right; it wouldn't hurt to give Maggie a call. The next day I called her at work. She seemed pleased when she realized it was me, which was a good sign. We decided to meet for lunch the following day.

We chose to eat at a small, outdoor, Mexican restaurant

across the street from the park near my apartment. I spent the morning sitting by the little stream, and then I walked over at our meeting time.

It was a warm August day, but there was a cool breeze which made the air pleasant. The sky was gorgeous – white puffy clouds everywhere against a bright blue background. I sat down at a table near the street to wait for Maggie. She arrived soon after I did, dressed in a pink and white sleeveless dress. Her dress, mixed with the cool breeze and the bounce in her step reminded me of springtime. She was even more striking than I had remembered.

"You look happy," I said in greeting.

"How could I not be, on a day such as this. Have you been waiting long?"

"No, I've been over in the park this morning; I just walked over here a minute or so ago."

"Good. Are you hungry? I'm starved."

About that time a waiter appeared. We quickly looked at the menu and ordered.

Then Maggie said, "I was glad you called yesterday."

"I felt a little funny calling you at work, but I hadn't thought to ask you for your home number."

"You just barely got me."

"What do you mean?" I asked.

"I'm changing jobs."

"How come?"

"It's a long story."

We spent the rest of our lunch talking about work, hers and mine. We talked as if we had known each other forever. It seemed to me that we had been together for only a few minutes before Maggie had to get back to work. I felt disappointed, wishing that we could have spent the whole afternoon together.

This time when I walked her to her car, I remembered to ask for her home phone number.

"Sure, let me write it down for you," she replied. When she handed it to me, she said, "There's something I need to tell you before you go, because I want to be straight up with you. If you decide not to call me again, I'll understand."

Her face was serious, and her tone matter-of-fact. I couldn't imagine what she was going to say that could be so important. Looking straight into her eyes, I waited patiently for her announcement.

Finally, she said, "I have two kids."

I grinned.

"What's so funny?" she asked.

"Is that all? I thought you were going to tell me something awful."

"So, that doesn't bother you?"

"No, should it? How old are they?"

"Michael's four and Samantha's six."

"A boy and a girl, huh?"

"Yeah, and they're quite a pair."

Then the ages of the children struck me. They were about the same age as Alex. "Four and six. Those are good ages… When do I get to meet them?"

"When do you want to?"

"How 'bout Friday night?"

"Okay. About six?"

"That'll be good," I replied.

It was so easy being with Maggie. In some ways she reminded me of Lynn, which was scary. But Maggie was older and seemed more mature and together than Lynn had been.

The next few days were interesting for me. I continued to step back and meditate my day, yet there was a new energy and excitement within me, as well. Never before had I been excited, yet calm and aware at the same time. It was a great combination.

By Friday evening, I was whistling Christmas tunes again. I whistled, "I'm dreaming of a white Christmas…" as I knocked on Maggie's front door.

Maggie lived in a tidy little two-story house. The house was grayish-blue with black shutters, and there were black window boxes full of red petunias under the front windows. The grass was freshly cut, and the flower beds looked as if they had been manicured.

No one came to the door at my first knock, so I knocked again. From inside, I heard a curious sounding voice say, "Nobody's home. Nobody's home."

Then I heard a child's voice, "I'll get it, Mom."

"Ask who it is before you open the door. His name is David," said a voice that sounded like Maggie's."

"Okay Mom... Who's there?" said the child's voice.

"It's David," I replied.

"It's him, Mom. Can I let him in?"

"Please. Let him on in."

The door opened and a delightful, little brown-haired girl stood before me.

"Mom says you can come in. She will be down in a minute."

As I entered the foyer, I heard, "Call the police! Call the police! Jail break! Jail break!" and from a room toward the back of the house came three large dogs and one small one, with a young boy running behind them.

"Jail break! Jail break! Call the police!" It was a shrill voice. I felt confused as the little girl showed me into the living room. To the right of the room, there was a flight of stairs which faced the foyer. To the left, there was a fireplace with a mantle. And flanking the fireplace were two large cages, each containing a parrot.

The parrot on the left cried, "Help me Mama. Help me," while the other one screamed, "Call the police! Jail break! Jail break!"

Meanwhile, the dogs were running, barking, and sliding on the hardwood floors as they chased each other around the sofa in the center of the room. It was a madhouse!

Then Maggie walked calmly down the steps as if nothing at all was happening. She was wearing a lavender dress with white lace trim. Her dress flattered her figure. Her hair was pulled to the the top of her head. She looked lovely.

As Maggie reached the midway point of the stairs, she said with authority, "Now hush, everyone of you!"

To my amazement, the dogs skidded to a halt and quit barking, and one of the parrots stopped talking. Immediately, the other one screamed, "Mama's here. Mama's here."

The little boy said, "Aw, Mom. It was like being at the circus."

Maggie replied, "Yes, it was. But it was a bit much, and you haven't met David yet. You and Samantha put the dogs out back, and then come right back in."

The small dog and one of the large ones came over to sniff me. Then the large one raised up on hind legs putting its front paws on my chest.

The little boy said, "Mama, Lady likes him."

I rubbed the dog's head, and it seemed that Lady smiled at me.

"She really likes that," offered the little boy. "She likes anyone that will rub her head."

Maggie said, "Just push her down if you don't want her on you." Then to the little boy, she said, "Go on now, Michael. Y'all put the dogs outside."

"Yes ma'am," he said, and he turned, leading the dogs through the kitchen toward the back door.

The little girl joined the small procession, clapping her hands and saying, "Come on doggies. Let's go." Eventually, they all disappeared out the back door.

The children were back in no time.

"David, this is Samantha, and this is Michael," said Maggie, as she put her arms around them and held them in front of her. "This is my friend, David," she said to them.

Neither of the children responded at first, and then Samantha said, "Nice to meet you."

From the look on her face, I guessed that she was assessing me and had not yet decided if I was all right or not.

"Do you like my mama?" asked Michael, taking me a bit off guard.

"Well… well, yes, I do like your mama," I said, grinning at Maggie.

Then one of the parrots said, "I'm a little bit'a heaven. I'm a love child."

I laughed. "Y'all have some mighty smart birds," I said to the kids.

"Do you like them?" Samantha asked.

"I certainly do."

"They can say anything," said Michael. "We teach 'em."

"They can even sing," said Samantha. "Do you want to hear 'em?"

"Sure."

"Get Freddy to sing, Mama," requested Samantha and Michael, almost in unison.

Maggie looked a bit embarrassed, even a little unsure of herself, which I hadn't seen before. But then her expression changed, and her determination and confidence returned.

"Come on Freddy, let's sing," she said, and then she began to sing, "I left my heart…"

Before she had finished saying, "heart," the bird took over, and sing he did, loud and clear, "I left my heart in San Francisco…"

The other bird started to sing as well, only it was a different song, "You are my sunshine, my only sunshine…" Samantha and Michael tried to get the second bird to stop, but there was no stopping her.

In the midst of the singing, there was a knock at the door. It was the babysitter.

"Okay kids, we've gotta go," said Maggie. "Hug me."

Maggie bent down to give each one of them a big hug.

"Now y'all be good for Wanda," said Maggie. "And Wanda, you know where everything is. You have my beeper number if you need me. We'll be back by 11:00 or so… And I'll see the two of you in the morning."

As we walked down the walkway to the car, Maggie said, "I hope that wasn't too much for you."

"It was kind of fun. I love animals, and your kids are great," I replied.

"Thanks. I think so, too, but I'm biased," she said, smiling.

I opened the car door for Maggie; then I went around to get

in myself.

"What do you want to eat?" I asked, sliding in behind the wheel.

"How 'bout pizza?" she said.

"That's fine with me."

Once we arrived, were seated, and had ordered, I said, "Seems like you've done a terrific job with your kids."

"I appreciate that. It hasn't been easy. They're a handful at times, especially Michael. Samantha's fairly easygoing, dependable, and grounded. I'm not sure I could have made it if she hadn't been, but Michael... he's another story. He's got more energy than anybody I've ever known, and he definitely has a mind of his own."

"I sensed that."

"You don't know the half of it," she said, shaking her head. "Let me tell you what he did a couple of weeks ago. He is always wanting to play in the creek behind our house or on the cul-de-sac, both of which I don't allow without supervision. Well, I caught him in the creek, and though I don't think spanking is the best form of discipline and rarely use it, I took him in the house and spanked him. You would have thought I had killed him he let out such a wail, and then he started crying those giant crocodile tears. I told him, 'I'm sorry for having to spank you, but I can't have you in that creek without an adult watching you. Do you understand? You know that we've talked about this many times.' He nodded his head, so I gave him a hug and told him to go on back out and play. Well, you're not going to believe what he did next. He started to walk out, but then he turned around and walked right back toward me; between sniffles, with tears still streaming down his face, he said, 'Mama, would you please just go ahead and whip me again, so I can go on back down to the creek?'"

I laughed and shook my head, "He's something else."

"Yes, he certainly is... And he can be so funny, sometimes... Like the other night, Samantha was trying to help him say his prayers before they went to bed. She always tries to get him to say, 'God, help me be a good boy,' but he won't say it. It wasn't until the other night that he finally gave in and met her halfway. He said, 'Okay God, help me be a good boy *some* of the time.'"

Again, I laughed. Maggie was a great storyteller, and it sounded as though she had endless volumes of material to draw from.

Then after a brief pause, I said, "It sounds like Michael and Samantha get along fairly well. Is that true?"

"Oh, yes. He thinks the world revolves around her, and she loves him to death. They are about as close as a brother and sister could be.

"And they take up for each other. Just last week, the little boy down the street was teasing Samantha, and Michael grabbed him around the leg and bit him. I punished him for biting the little boy, but inside I was kind of proud of him for standing up for his sister.

"The only problem is that sometimes Samantha will let Michael run over her. She lets him get away with things he shouldn't. Michael is rough, and he sometimes breaks Samantha's toys, but no matter how much I tell her to get after him, she won't. And then when I go to scold him for what he did, she starts crying and says, 'Please don't punish him, Mama. He's my little brother. He didn't mean to.'"

I said, "Just count yourself fortunate if that's the biggest problem you have with them. It's not like that in most families."

"I know," she replied. "We're pretty close. I try to spend as much time with them as I can, especially since they don't have a father."

"What happened to him? If you don't mind my asking."

"I don't mind. My husband died in a car accident right after Michael was born. A drunk driver hit him – crossed over the median and hit him head on. They said he died instantly."

"I'm sorry."

"Me, too. But, it's not so bad, now. At first, it was tough raising two kids by myself, but things have really improved over the last year or so."

She paused, and then said, "You know... I was looking forward to hearing more about you this evening, and here I've done all the talking. I've sat here and talked about my kids the whole time. I've just rattled on and on."

"I've enjoyed hearing about them."

"But I want to hear about you. What do you like to do?"

"Well..." I said and then I paused in thought before continuing, "I like to run, and I like to play golf."

She smiled at that and said, "Me, too, about the running. I've never played golf, but how far do you run?"

"Usually about three miles."

"I'm not quite up to that yet. I've only been running for about three months, now, but I'll run a couple with you sometime, if you want. I don't run very fast, though."

"That's okay, me neither... What else can I tell you about me?... I take aikido. It's a form of martial arts. Also, I like to spend a fair amount of time alone. And I especially enjoy sitting beside this small stream near my apartment. How 'bout you? What do you enjoy?"

She silently considered my question and then replied, "I enjoy my time alone, too, but I don't get much of it – mostly after the kids have gone to bed. I work out two or three times a week, either running or at the gym. Probably my favorite thing to do is to watch good movies."

"What kind of movies?"

"All kinds, except horror movies. I especially like detective shows and movies that make me think."

"I enjoy a good movie now and then myself, and I like the ones that make me think, too."

Our waitress brought our pizza, and it was superb, with an abundance of cheese and sauce. The evening went as well as it could have until Maggie said, "David, there's a guy over there who keeps staring at us."

I turned my head to look, and there was Brian. When he saw me look his way, he smiled and waved. I didn't know what to do, so I waved back.

"Is he a friend of yours?" Maggie asked.

"No, not hardly," I replied.

"He seems glad to see you."

"I'm not glad to see him."

While we ate, I told Maggie about Lynn and Brian, glancing over at Brian every now and then as I spoke. In the midst of the story, Brian finished eating and left. I was glad to see him go.

His presence concerned me, but I was determined not to let it cloud the evening. The rest of the evening went well, including saying good-bye to Maggie at her front door. I felt like a nervous schoolboy as I wrestled with whether or not to kiss her good night. Finally, I reached over and gave her a soft kiss on the lips. As I pulled away, a question crossed my mind, so I asked it.

"I've never asked anyone this before," I said, "But did my mustache feel prickly when I kissed you?"

"I didn't notice," she replied, "Let me see."

Then she placed her hands on the sides of my face and pulled my mouth to hers. After a long, passionate kiss, she said, "No, it's not prickly in the least. It's soft."

"Good," I replied, a bit dazed.

Maggie smiled and said, "Call me," and then she turned and walked inside.

12 Contentment

The last few weeks of the summer were wonderful. Maggie and I saw a lot of each other, but I still continued to spend a great deal of time alone.

Maggie had a life of her own. She was not at all demanding of my time. We both seemed to love each other's company, but neither of us seemed super possessive for which I was grateful.

Our relationship felt healthy. It was the first time I had ever been in a relationship that I didn't fall head over heels and want to be with the girl or woman every moment of every day. There was a balance to our relationship that felt good. It felt right.

I began the new school year, my third year at Fair Hope, with renewed vigor and a heightened sense of creativity. My vacation had done its job. I was looking forward to getting back to work.

It was great to see everyone again: Mr. Franklin, Mrs. Tyson, and my students. There was something missing from the aura of the school, however. Things were just not the same without Christine. A new school coordinator, a Mrs. McDonald, had been hired. She seemed nice enough, but she wasn't Christine. Still, life had to go on, and so it did.

Over the last few weeks of the summer, Maggie and I had gone out primarily alone, but as school began, we decided to do some things with her children. We planned to make the Labor Day weekend a fun-filled family event, spending Saturday at the park, Sunday at the zoo, and topping the weekend off with a cookout at Maggie's on Monday evening. Saturday was a day of swings, merry-go-rounds, slides, and games of tickle and chase, topped off with ice cream cones from the nearby Dairy Queen. Michael loved to swing, and he insisted on my being his pusher. Of course, Samantha wanted me to push her, too, so I took turns. Maggie thought it was funny, teasing me from her seat on a nearby bench, "You're not getting tired, are you?" she said. "You'd better conserve your energy; Michael can swing all day long."

On Sunday, I picked up Alex on my way to Maggie's so he could join us on our zoo adventure. I was a little anxious about how he and Maggie's kids would get along, but I soon found that I had nothing to worry about. When we arrived at Maggie's, Samantha took over. She showed Alex their parrots and had the birds sing for him. He was amazed. Then both children took Alex to the backyard to meet their dogs. By the time we got in the car to go to the zoo, they were fast friends.

"I want to see the snakes," said Alex.

"Not me," said Samantha. "I don't like snakes; they're too slimy."

"I want to see the baby elephants," said Michael.

"What are we going to see first, Mama?" asked Samantha.

"I don't know what we'll see first," replied Maggie. "We'll just have to wait until we get there."

"How much longer?" asked Michael, already tired of riding.

"We'll be there in about ten minutes," I replied.

Once we had purchased tickets and entered the park, the kids ran straight to the first animals they saw – the lions. After a brief discussion about the fact that lions weren't like people because "the boy lions had long hair and the girl lions had short hair," the kids were off to look at the baboons.

"They're full of energy today," I said to Maggie.

"They really are excited," she said, "but they'll slow down a little before too long… I hope."

When we caught up with the children, I heard Michael say, "He has a bald fanny."

"And it's pink," said Alex.

Maggie and I shared a laugh – until the baboon gave us a mean look, as if he knew we were laughing at him.

"He's getting mad at us," said Samantha, as she backed away from the railing.

"It's okay," said Alex. "He can't get us."

During the next hour or so, we saw elephants, tigers, deer, and spider monkeys. Michael was thrilled with the baby elephants and started copying them, acting as if one of his arms were a trunk. When the little elephant grabbed onto its mother's tail, Michael grabbed the back of Maggie's shorts. At first Maggie tried to get away, but then she gave in to play the role of the mama elephant, swinging her right arm in front of her face as Michael was doing. Samantha, Alex, and I could not help but laugh as we watched Maggie and Michael in their elephant drama.

In the end, it was the spider monkeys that stole the show. There was one young monkey who reminded me a lot of Michael. He was constantly scampering around bothering the other monkeys and getting into trouble.

He stole a banana from one of the older females and took off. The other monkeys would not let him near their food, so he took a brief time out in one corner to eat his banana. Then he threw the peel up in the air, taking off on a hysterical run through every inch of free space in the cage, swinging from limb to limb as he went. There was an abundance of squealing and quite a few feats of athleticism, such as flips off the trapeze that was hanging from the top of the cage. Of course, his antics were an inspiration for the kids, who imitated with running, squealing, and jumping of their own.

Maggie and I stood and watched for a few moments, but when we realized that the children were so totally captivated, we took the opportunity to rest on one of the nearby benches.

"I haven't been to the zoo in a long time," I said to Maggie.

"Yes, it's fun, isn't it? And not as hot as I thought it would be. This breeze is nice."

"It certainly is."

After a few moments of silence, Maggie said, "Children are

so amazing. They see everything through eyes of wonder. Everything is new and fascinating. They help me see the wonder more myself. Maybe that's why Jesus said that we have to be like little children if we want to enter the kingdom of heaven."

"They sure look like they're in heaven," I responded.

As we watched them and the monkeys, I thought about what Maggie had said. The children, especially Michael, who was the youngest, saw the world through simple, uncomplicated eyes. His body and mind weren't full of the tension and anxiety which was so characteristic of our society. His thoughts were not filled with hopes and dreams of the future or regrets of the past. He was free to live in the present moment.

That is heaven, I thought. We are born experiencing heaven, and then day by day, as we grow older and supposedly *smarter*, we lose it. We lose the magic and the mystery. Our efforts to be somebody, to succeed, to fix everything and everyone, to avoid death, failure, pain, and all that we have categorized as unpleasant, lead us further and further away from what we're really after.

Still, heaven never really leaves us. It's always there.

"Hey, where'd you go?" asked Maggie, bringing me back to the reality of the moment.

"I was just thinking about what you said about the children and heaven," I replied, and then for no apparent reason, I glanced to my left. There was Brian about twenty yards away from us, standing beside the tiger cage. He was dressed in navy blue shorts and a white polo shirt. He was looking our way.

Maggie turned and saw him, too.

"It's him again," she said.

"Maggie, I have an uneasy feeling about seeing him again."

"It doesn't seem right, does it?" she answered. "But there's not much we can do about it."

"I think he's up to something," I replied. "We need to be careful and keep our eyes open."

"And trust," she said quietly as if she were saying it more to herself than to me.

When I looked back toward the tiger cage, Brian was gone. I looked all around, but there was no sign of him anywhere.

Though I knew intuitively that Brian was up to no good, Maggie was right. All we could do was "trust," stay aware, and handle things the best we knew how.

We spent the remainder of the afternoon enjoying the radiant sunshine, the bright blue sky, and the variety of amusing animals all around us. We didn't see Brian anymore, and thoughts of him gradually faded away.

After leaving the zoo, we stopped for a bite to eat at a small cafeteria, and then we stopped at a grocery store on the way home to pick up some items for our Labor Day cookout. It had been a long day, and I was surprised at the energy the kids still had. They were wide-eyed and virtual chatterboxes as we trooped through the store aisles. After collecting all we needed and passing through the checkout line, we headed back to the van. It was dark now.

"Okay, kids. Let's hold hands," said Maggie, and off we marched across the parking lot. I was pushing the cart with Maggie, Michael, Alex, and Samantha holding hands in a line beside me. The van was parked on the right side of the lot toward the end of the row, underneath one of the brightly-lit parking lot lights.

When we were just a few yards from the van, Samantha let go of Alex's hand and ran toward the van. Alex took off after her. Michael tried to follow, but Maggie wouldn't let him go.

"No, you stay here with me," Maggie said to Michael as he tried to shake loose.

Just as Samantha was about to reach the van, a figure slid out from behind a nearby truck and yanked Samantha up into his arms. It was Brian.

Maggie gasped and started to move toward them, but I grabbed her. Alex moved slowly away from Brian and Samantha, edging back toward us.

Brian said, "Stay where you are."

We were about five or six yards away from him and Samantha. He held Samantha in his right arm and a gun in his left. The gun was pointed our way.

"You took my Lynn away from me. You screwed up my life," he sneered, "and now I'm going to mess up yours. I've been waiting for just the right time. You're going to pay. I'm gonna take this little girl. Your girlfriend there will never forgive you, because it'll be your fault. She'll never love you now. She will always blame you for her little girl being gone."

He began to ease away from the van, saying, "Don't try to be a hero," as he waved the gun my way. "I wouldn't mind shooting you, so don't try me."

About that time, Michael, who had been standing beside Maggie, broke loose from her grasp and took off running towards Brian.

"You can't take my sister!" he yelled.

Alex took off right behind him.

Brian looked bewildered and at a loss about what to do. At first, he pointed the gun at the boys, but then he remembered Maggie and me, and he pointed it back at us. Michael wrapped himself around Brian's leg and bit into his calf, sinking his sharp teeth deep into the large man's leg.

"Ouugh!" screamed Brian, as he tried to kick Michael away, but the little boy held on tight. "Damn it, get off my leg!" he yelled.

Alex grabbed Samantha's legs in an attempt to pull her free. Brian shoved Alex away with the back of his gun hand. Alex went sprawling to the pavement. Michael still held fast. Brian continued trying to kick Michael off his leg. Then he stumbled. That was the opening I needed. Before Brian could regain his balance, I was on him, grabbing his gun hand at the wrist. His right arm still held Samantha, so it was of no use to him. As we struggled for the gun, it went off. The bullet entered the side of a nearby car.

I lifted his arm into the air and slammed it against the top edge of the back of the van. The gun fired a second time. Again, I slammed his wrist against the van. This time, the gun went flying over the top of the van.

Brian threw Samantha to the ground and grabbed me around

the neck in a forearm choke hold. I let go of his left arm to grab
at his right, which felt as though it were crushing my throat. I
felt faint and gasped for air.

"Let go of him!" screamed Maggie. She tackled Brian, knocking us both against the back of the van. My head hit hard
against the metal door. I couldn't see – all was a blur. But hitting the van had loosened Brian's grasp on my neck. I could
breathe now. The faint feeling subsided, and though I couldn't
see, I knew I had to do something. My instincts and training
took over. Quickly, I turned and elbowed Brian in the side.

"Uunh!" escaped from his lips.

I elbowed him again.

"Uunh!" he repeated. This time his arm loosened and lowered a bit. I pushed us both away from the van. I turned to my
left, stepped behind his right leg with my left, threw my arms
up toward his face, and leaned back into him. He tripped and
fell to the pavement with a thud, pulling me down on top of
him. He rolled to the left and threw me off his chest. I scampered to my feet, still not able to see clearly. I moved my head
to the left and to the right, hoping to discern anything that
would let me know his location.

Maggie screamed, and I thought Brian must be after her or
one of the kids. Then I felt a crushing blow to my left eye that
sent me sprawling back against a car. I rolled to my right, figuring that Brian would follow the blow with another. And
immediately after moving, I heard him crashing against the car
I had just left.

As I turned again to face him, an inexplicable calmness came
over me. I was blind and in great danger, yet I was calm.

Brian reached for me, and though I couldn't see his hands, I
somehow knew exactly where they were. My body took over,
as if it were being directed by something other than my mind.
I reached for his wrists as his hands were coming toward my
throat. With both of his wrists in my grasp, I made a quick twist
of my body to the left, hitting him in the stomach with my left
hip. He flipped over my shoulder and hit the pavement.

I heard Brian scrambling to his feet. Then I heard, "Stop!" in another man's voice.

Brian took off running.

"He's over there," someone cried.

"Where?" another voice yelled.

"Running toward the street," screamed the first voice. There was shouting, running footsteps, commotion. A horn blew. Suddenly above the noise, I heard the terrible sound of screeching tires and an impact. Then there was silence. Everything came to a standstill.

"Oh my God," cried Maggie and she buried her head in my chest.

"What happened?" I asked, although I felt I knew.

"He got hit by a car as he was running from the security guard," said Maggie.

"Brian?" I asked.

"Yeah… It was awful," she said.

I held Maggie close to me. "Are you okay?" I asked.

"I'm fine, and the kids seem okay, too," she replied. "How about you?"

"Yeah, I'm fine… but crazy as it sounds, I feel kind of sad."

"What do you mean?"

"Brian was so miserable… so filled with hate. It was his hate that did him in. And that's sad."

"Are you sure you're okay?" repeated Maggie, probably wondering how I could be worrying about Brian when he had just tried to kill me.

"Yeah, I'm fine," I reassured her. "I really am. My vision's blurry, but other than that, I'm okay."

I felt a pair of tiny arms wrap around my waist and then another pair around my left leg. It was Alex and Michael.

"You really got that bad man, Uncle David," said Alex.

I rubbed his head with my hand. I didn't know what to say. Brian wasn't bad – no more than the rest of us. Unhappy and lost, maybe. Very lost. He had placed all of his worth in another person's love, and when that love was withdrawn, it had made him crazy. But Alex didn't need to hear all that.

All I could think to say was, "Alex, Brian was a very

unhappy person. And yes, he did some bad things."

After we talked with the police, and the rescue team checked us over, Maggie drove us to her house. We called Jenny to tell her what had happened, and though we assured her that Alex was fine, she came straight over to see for herself. When she arrived, she found the kids reenacting the fight, each giving their version of what had happened. They were jumping around, throwing fake punches, and falling to the ground as they took turns playing different roles. None of them wanted to be Brian, but since the drama was no good without a Brian, they decided to take turns playing his "bad guy" part.

It had been an incredibly long day. I was exhausted, but I stayed at Maggie's until almost midnight, rehashing the evening's events while I waited for my vision to clear so I could drive home. Once home, I plopped in bed without even taking off my clothes or washing up first. I couldn't remember ever having been so tired, and I immediately fell asleep. In my dreams I found myself walking beside a crystal stream. I felt a strong sense of connection with the stream, as if it were a part of me. As I strolled along admiring the clear rippling water, beautiful multi-colored flowers began to pop up, one after another, all around me. Each flower displayed the colors of the rainbow. The scene was so tranquil and alluring that I decided to postpone my journey and sit for a while at the stream's edge.

After a soothing rest, I continued on my journey, my path leading me into a forest of enormous, dark trees. It looked foreboding, yet I was not afraid. I knew only peace as I strolled along my path. The sound of crunching leaves under my feet created a joyous melody that accompanied me on my way. Rays of sunshine shone through the large massive branches, lighting my path. I couldn't tell for sure, but it seemed that the limbs were moving aside to enable the light to shine through and show me the way. Now and then, I would see squirrels darting in and out of the light as they chased one another overhead. Hundreds of birds sang in the shadows. It was a pleasant walk, and I was enjoying it immensely.

All of a sudden, I realized that I was aware though in a

dream. I was struck by the similarities between my present dream and my first dream. I had heard of lucid dreams, dreams in which one is conscious while being asleep, yet I had never experienced one. It felt strange being cognizant while also being asleep.

After walking for a short while through the dense forest, I came upon an enormous grayish-brown wall. It was the same wall that I had encountered in my first dream. Gazing at the endless mass of stone, I thought back to my other dreams, the golden book, and what I had learned since then. Once again, the wall stood ominously unmoving before me. Again, it was blocking my path. But this time it didn't seem to matter. This time I decided to sit and experience the moment, to let the silence caress me as I faced what appeared to be the end of my journey.

Before long, I heard the sound of crunching leaves behind me. It was Brian, but I felt no fear. He casually strolled up and sat down beside me. Soon, others joined us. First, there was Lynn and Mrs. Tyson, and then two fellows that I didn't recognize until Brian whispered, "Those are the treasure hunters who broke into your apartment." More and more people came up and sat with us; each one was a person who had brought unpleasantness to my life.

Few words were spoken. Mostly, we just sat content with the tranquil stillness of the moment.

As I gazed at the wall, questions began to fill my mind: What's the deal here? Why is this wall in my dreams again? Why is it blocking my path? What am I supposed to be learning from this experience? Or am I just here to experience, and there's nothing for me to learn from this?

In the past, my mind would have been scrambling to find the answers, but not this day. Instead, I sat quietly aware of the questions. Then out of the silence came an answer: "The wall is not blocking your path. It is part of your path, just as the people sitting around you have been part of your path. Each one of them, just like the wall, has played a part in your growth and your development."

Okay, I thought to myself, if I need to sit at this wall, that's fine with me. And then out loud to the Oneness, I said, "Thy will be done!"

As those words came from my lips, I heard a twinkling sound. A door appeared in the center of the wall. It opened slowly. A bright light shown through the opening, causing all of us to hide our eyes until they adjusted to the brightness.

I heard these words in my mind, "It's time for you to enter."

Rising from the ground, I walked to the doorway. I turned back to the others, motioning for them to come with me, but they stood fast, saying, "It's not our time yet, but one day we will join you." They were smiling.

Within, I knew that they were right. There were many journeys ahead of them, but yes, one day they would join me. At peace with the reality of the moment, I turned and walked through the door.

The light was even brighter on the other side, and again I was blinded. I felt as if I were being consumed by the brilliance. In time my eyes adapted, and I saw that I was in a large room. A gigantic potter's wheel stood in the center of the room. From the base up, it stood over six feet tall, and the wheel itself was twenty-five feet in diameter.

Granddad was standing beside the wheel with his two friends in white.

Granddad said, "Contentment is found in the center of the wheel. For it is only when you are in the center that you can stand without being thrown to and fro. So it is with life. Only when you are in a state of balance, in the center of the bull's-eye, can you stand against the extremes that life throws your way.

"The golden book is in the center of the wheel."

Over to the left of the wheel was a set of steps, which I climbed to get to the top of the wheel. From my new vantage point, the wheel looked like a giant target colored in black and white concentric rings with a red bull's-eye for its center. And in the middle of the bull's-eye was the golden book shining brightly, as it had in all of my other dreams.

As I stepped out onto the wheel to get the book, the wheel started to turn, slowly at first, but then faster and faster. I began to lose my balance, staggering as the centrifugal force pulled me toward the edge of the rapidly spinning wheel. I tried desperately to regain my balance, finally dropping to my hands and knees in an attempt to steady myself, but it was too late. I flew off the wheel and hit the ground, rolling head over heels. When I tried to stand up, I found myself feeling dizzy and disoriented.

After my bearings were restored, I climbed the steps again to give the wheel another try. This time, however, I took a much more cautious approach by starting off on my hands and knees. But even that was not enough. Finally, I lay flat on my stomach and inched my way toward the center. By the time I reached the middle, I was extremely dizzy. Then after just a few moments in the center, I began to realize that it felt different in the center of the wheel. The centrifugal force was powerless against me there, and somehow spinning in the center did not create as much dizziness. I could even stand up.

I stood in the middle of the spinning wheel for a brief time, and then I sat down and opened the golden book.

Many
begin
their
spiritual journeys
by seeking to love,
but as long as one is thrown
to and fro
by desires and attachments,
truly loving others
is not possible.

*W*ithout a foundation
   of trust, openness,
      and understanding,
      love becomes distorted by
   selfishness and other perversions.

*N*ow that
      you have a better grasp
         of who you are,
         and you have
      traveled the path to oneness,
   you are ready to learn about
      and experience real love...

... *A love that is
      unconditional,
         freeing,
            and nonjudgmental;*

*A love that is so powerful
      that when it touches another,
   it frees that person
      from the illusions
         that bind.*

But you must not strive for this love.

*Instead,
      open to it,
   and let yourself be filled to
         overflowing,
   and let the love within you
      flow out and touch
         all who come near you.*

Remember,
things
are
always
simpler
than they seem.

The divine potter
is spinning the wheel;
the universe is molding you
and making you
into what you were created to be:
your true self.

Your part in the process is to trust,
listen within to that still, small voice,
and stay balanced
in the center of the wheel.

I awoke at 6:55 A.M., stood up and stretched. The sun streamed through my bedroom window. I sensed a fine day ahead.

Somehow, life felt more real than before, as if my life up until that point had been just a dream, and now the dream was over. There was a lightness in the air. Everything seemed brighter and clearer. I felt as if I had been looking at life through dark glasses and had finally removed them.

I walked to the kitchen, poured a glass of orange juice, and went out on my balcony. Even the juice tasted better than usual. I spent the next hour or so enjoying the morning, sipping juice, and recording my dream in my journal. Then I went for a walk. A slight, knowing smile crept to my face as I strolled along the sidewalks and through the streets. Content and empty, experiencing only what was before me, I walked aimlessly along, taking in the heaven around me.

After walking for about forty-five minutes, I headed home. On the way, I wandered down Granddad's street wishing that he were around so I could tell him my tale. As I approached his house, I was delighted to find him sitting in his front yard with a drink in hand and an empty chair beside him.

"I've been waiting for you," he said.

"When did you get back?" I asked as I crossed the lawn.

"Last night. I was tempted to come to the grocery parking lot and watch, but I decided to wait until this morning to see you."

"So you know about Brian?"

"And Maggie and the dream," he replied. "Yep, I know about most everything that has happened in the last twenty-four hours, but I would like to hear about what you've experienced since I've been gone. What have you learned since we last talked?"

"Quite a bit," I replied. "I'm not sure I know where to begin."

Granddad waited in silence.

"It wasn't easy, Granddad," I finally said. "At first, I had a really hard time just staying focused. Once I got a hold on that, life began to feel better for a while. But then, all of a sudden, out of nowhere, I found myself depressed – *very* depressed. Looking back on it now, I think the depression came as a result of my letting go of some of my old ways, my old thoughts, and my old views of reality.

"You would think that seeing things more clearly and letting go of erroneous beliefs would have made me feel better. It didn't at first. I went through a period of pure hell, before I came out of it and started to feel better.

"My life's pretty much flowed along since then. Until yesterday. But you know, I still have one question. I don't think anyone can really answer it, but I'd like to know your opinion. Granddad, why do you think we're here? What's our purpose?"

"I think you're right," said Granddad. "No one knows for sure why we're here, and anyone who thinks he knows is probably kidding himself. But if I were to give a guess, and that's all it would be... I'd say that once upon a time, all that existed was the Oneness. Then came the creation of human beings. Humans were given a priceless gift – the gift of freedom, the gift of individuality, the gift of personhood. But with that gift, also came separateness, which when you break it down, adds up to the loss of the experience of oneness. The gift of individuality is a great and wonderful gift, but the acceptance of that gift, as you can see, has its downside.

"So I would say that life is about experiencing our separateness. It's about finding out who we are. It's about living in the now and experiencing the truth of our situation."

"And what is the truth of our situation?" I asked.

"The truth is that we are part of the Oneness, yet separate from it at the same time," said Granddad. "Life is about realizing and living this truth. It's about the bringing together of apparent opposites. It's about learning to be separate and one at the same time. It's about regaining our experience of oneness, while still keeping our sense of individuality. Life is about learning how to live interdependently with others who are part of us, yet separate from us, all at once. So really, life is about togetherness. It's about love."

Then Granddad paused, as if he were waiting for me to respond.

After a few moments of consideration, I said, "What you're saying makes sense, but if you're right, then we humans still have a long way to go. There's still so much selfishness in the world."

"You're right; we do have a long way to go. But that's okay. Even the selfishness is okay. It's part of the process. Remember, everyone is doing the best he can in light of his situation. We all have to move through the selfishness phase before we realize that it doesn't pay off for us, that it doesn't get us what we want. We all have to find emptiness before we can find true fullness. Learning to trust the process and live through the emptiness, as you've found out, is not an easy thing to do."

"No, it's not," I said. "I've spent most of my life trying to fill the emptiness within me. I've tried to fill it with anything and everything: schoolwork, golf, tennis, basketball, part time jobs, girlfriends, friendships, anything that would take away the pain, anything that would take away the loneliness, even if for only a moment. Essentially, everything I have done has been an attempt to fill myself up. I didn't know that true fullness was not going to come until after I passed through the emptiness and faced the reality of myself."

"And until you let go of your false self," Granddad added.

"You know, Granddad, that was one of the most difficult parts for me, especially in the beginning. I'd always been afraid of that phrase: 'You have to lose your life, if you want to find it.'

"The reality of losing one's life is nothing like I thought it would be. I was afraid that losing my life would mean losing my awareness of self and others, that I would lose my consciousness – lose the part of me that knows, enjoys, plays, and feels, and that life would no longer be worth living. I was afraid that if I lost myself I would no longer be me anymore, and for quite a while, that was more than I was willing to risk."

Granddad sat quietly listening, that slight knowing smile on his face.

"But it's not that way at all," I continued. "The part of me that I've lost and that I'm still losing is not really me. It is my ego. It's that part of me which came into being when my eternal self entered this finite world. It is nothing more than a mirror image of all my experiences, my needs, the things I've learned, and even some of the aspects of my personality. It is an extension of me, but it's not who I am. It's not me.

"All of my fears, my beliefs, my needs to strive and succeed, and my needs to feel secure and to like myself – all are ego related and have very little to do with my real self. The real me is the part of me that experiences. It's the part of me that observes my thoughts and my feelings; it's the part that watches myself as I relate to others. I am the part of me that I can't see."

I paused for a few seconds before continuing.

"You know, Granddad, I see a lot of things differently, now," and then I paused again. "I used to spend much of my energy trying to do good things because I wanted others to see me as good, and because I wanted to believe it about myself. Now I realize that's not how it works at all. Good actions don't create goodness. Good actions *come* from goodness. We are all good deep down inside, but some of us have forgotten that truth. All of our thoughts, hurts, and insecurities get in our way and prevent us from seeing reality. They lead us to imbalance and self-centeredness.

"And until we get past our selfishness and learn to seek the highest good for all concerned, we won't ever experience real love. Until we regain our balance and learn to listen within for directions, we won't know if what we're doing is truly the loving thing to do or not.

"When we first started, I couldn't help but wonder where love, compassion, and giving fit into what you were teaching me. Everything you had me do seemed so self-centered. But now it makes sense. After realizing who we are and our true place in the universe, we can't help but be compassionate, loving, and giving because those qualities are part of the fiber of our being. They are part of who we are."

"You've come a long way," said Granddad.

"I guess I have," I replied.

"Well tell me, David. Has it been worth it? Was the journey worth the trouble?"

"No doubt about it!" I said. "Though it was difficult, and I wasn't always sure that I was going to make it, I'd do it again if I had to. Yeah, no doubt in my mind. It was well worth it."

Granddad and I spent the rest of the morning together, but it was different from before. Instead of talking about life, we just lived it, one moment at a time.

*   *   *

Sometimes when people go through an emotionally-packed event together, a closeness develops that bonds them forever. That seemed to be what happened with Maggie, Samantha, Michael, Alex, and me. After the attack in the parking lot, we became a somewhat inseparable team. The three children wanted to be together every minute they could, and I started spending more time at Maggie's than at my own apartment. With each passing day, I began to feel more and more like Samantha's and Michael's father. Halloween came, and we trick-or-treated together. Christmas Eve came, and Maggie and I stayed up all night putting toys together: a race track, a doll house, and a wagon. I enjoyed every minute of our time together – the piggy back rides, the stories at bedtime, and the time with Maggie after the kids were asleep. I was as content as I could be.

Toward the end of January, I found myself thinking a great deal about marriage, and finally I asked Maggie to marry me. She said, "Yes."

The wedding was planned for the week of spring break. Maggie and I could both be off then, and the kids could stay with their grandma while we were on our honeymoon. We spent much of February and March preparing for the wedding. It wasn't to be a big wedding, but as everyone knows, weddings seem to take on a life of their own, often growing way beyond one's original intentions. We had to decide where to have the service, what kind of cake to have, and what kind of finger foods to serve. There seemed to be hundreds of decisions to be made and thousands of things to do.

Since we were planning to live at Maggie's after we were married, I had to move from my apartment. With school, aikido, and the preparation for the wedding happening all at once, I was not able to move until the weekend before the wedding.

It was a dazzling spring day. The sun was shining brightly. There was a cool breeze blowing in from the north and not a cloud to be seen.

Jenny came over to help us. She and Maggie packed boxes, while Alex, Samantha, and Michael played with Alex's cars in the walk-in closet. It was the perfect place for them to play, because it was cozy, like a playhouse, and it also kept them from under our feet.

Maggie's brother Jim and I did the moving. We moved most of the larger items on Saturday while the women were packing. Afterwards, we loaded the boxes, leaving just a few smaller items and some cleaning for Sunday.

On Sunday, while Jenny and Maggie cleaned and the kids played with their cars in the closet, I loaded the truck with the few remaining items. I had just finished putting the last lamp on the truck when Jenny and Maggie came down the steps with their cleaning supplies in hand.

"Look at you out here loafing, letting us women do all the work," teased Maggie, and then she kissed me on the cheek and said, "All we've got left to do is drag the kids from their closet playhouse, close up, and go home. We're done. You get the kids. We'll meet you at the house."

"All right. See y'all in a few minutes," I replied, and then I started up the stairs to round up the children.

As I ascended the steps, I thought back to the day I had moved in. So much had happened since then. The last few years had been full of surprises.

Stepping into the closet where the kids were playing, I said, "Time to go, y'all. Let's pick up these cars."

"Aw, do we have to?" They groaned in unison.

"Sure do. Here, I'll help you," I replied, as I squatted down, picked up a couple of cars, and put them in one of Alex's model car cases. But when I went to pick up a few more, my attention was drawn to two dump trucks. Each was filled with what appeared to be diamonds and rubies. I sat down in disbelief.

"Where did you get these?" I asked, picking up a couple of the jewels from one of the trucks, showing them to the kids.

"Out of this green bag," said Alex. He held up a small drawstring bag of green felt.

"Where did the bag come from?"

"Out of the wall," he replied. The other two children were silent.

"Out of the wall?" I questioned. "What do you mean?"

"Michael was crashing one of the cars into the wall like it was having a wreck," explained Alex. "When he did, a tiny door in the wall opened, and this green bag fell out."

"Show me."

"We closed it back," said Samantha.

"I'll show you," said Michael, going over to the wall. He hit against it a couple of times with one of the cars, and just as Alex had said, one of the panels in the wall fell open.

"A secret compartment," I said aloud to myself.

"Did we do something wrong?" asked Samantha. "Are we in trouble?"

"No, not in the least," I answered, smiling.

We picked up the cars, put the jewels back in the small green pouch, locked the door to the apartment, and headed down to the car. Waiting for us at the foot of the stairs was Granddad.

"You all moved out?" he asked.

"Yep," I said, "and we just got a big surprise as we finished."

I turned to the kids, saying, "Why don't y'all go down to the shady end of the porch and play with your cars some more while I talk with Granddad a minute?"

That was fine with them. In no time at all they were again totally engrossed in play.

"Granddad, look at these," I said, as I handed him the bag of jewels.

"Wow!" he exclaimed, after pouring some of the jewels into his hand. "Where'd you get these?"

"The kids found them in my apartment."

"These are worth a lot of money," he said. "A *lot* of money!"

I told Granddad the story about the millionaire and the jewels, and he laughed and then asked, "So what are you going to do with 'em?"

"First, I'll have to talk to the woman who owns the building and see if she's true to her word – that 'anyone who finds jewels in this building can have them.' I don't know what I'll do

after that. You know, it's kind of ironic. My whole life I've wanted to be rich, until just recently. And now when riches don't
really matter to me anymore, here they are. Isn't that weird? It's
almost like wanting more actually gets you less."

"That's often true," replied Granddad.

About that time, Granddad's cardinal friend landed on his
shoulder.

"Hey, fella," said Granddad to the bird. "Did you come to see
me off?"

"See you off?" I questioned.

"Yeah, I came to tell you bye," he replied.

"Where are you headed?"

"Back to the mountains."

"When will you be back?"

"I don't know. My job here is done for now. I've sublet my
house."

"You're moving?" I asked, surprised, but still much more at
ease than the last time Granddad had said he was going away.

"Yeah, I met a new student while I was gone, and it's about
time to get back to her."

I didn't know what to say. Granddad had shown up out of
nowhere and helped me totally change my view of life. Now he
was leaving much as he had come, in the blink of an eye. I
guess I shouldn't have been surprised. That was Granddad; he
was following his gut.

"I'll miss you," I said. "Thanks for all you've done, for stick-
ing with me the whole way."

"It wasn't me. I didn't do it," he said. "You did. And what do
you mean, 'the whole way?' You don't think your journey's
over, do ya?"

"No,... I mean up 'til now. I know it's not over. I figure as
long as I'm still alive, there is more to learn and more enlight-
ening experiences ahead of me."

"That's pretty much the truth of it. If you're still here, you're
not done." Then he paused before saying, "Well, I guess I need
to get on. Let me give you a hug."

When he moved toward me, the cardinal on his shoulder

took off.

I could feel my eyes beginning to tear up as we hugged. Granddad meant a lot to me.

We said, "Good-bye," and Granddad turned to walk away. As he did, his cardinal friend reappeared. The cardinal did a few loops and twists and then flew around Granddad's head a couple of times.

"See you, little fella," he said, as the bird did an elegant spin to the left. Then it spiraled up in the air and glided down past Granddad one more time.

Granddad waved to me and I waved back. I knew it was probably going to be a long time before I would see him again.

As I lowered my arm, I felt something touch my left shoulder. When I looked to see what it was, there sat the cardinal. I grinned from ear to ear and turned to show Granddad, only to find him laughing and shaking his head from side to side.

"How about that!" he yelled.

At that moment the kids distracted my attention as they came running toward me, yelling and screaming. They were very excited and talking all at once. Surprisingly, the cardinal stayed on my shoulder as the children clamored around me.

Before giving my full attention to the children, I turned back toward Granddad, waving bye one last time. Then to the children I said, "Slow down,… now one at a time."

"Uncle David," said Alex. "There's a red bird sitting on your shoulder."

"How 'bout that," I replied.

"Can you get him to sit on my shoulder?" asked Samantha.

"That's between you and the red bird," I said, glancing at the cardinal.

"How did you get him to come to you?" asked Alex.

"That's a long story," I said. "One day, when you're a little older, I'll have to tell you all about it. But right now, let's go home."

ABOUT THE AUTHOR

Robert Hudson lives in Birmingham, Alabama. He is available for lectures and workshops on spiritual growth, finding and living your path, relaxation and meditation, and managing stress and burnout.

He can be contacted through Enlightened Quest Publishing.

Write to: **Robert Hudson**
c/o Enlightened Quest Publishing
P. O. Box 11692
Birmingham, Alabama 35202

ORDER FORM

Please send _____ copies
of **The Center of the Wheel** at $13.95 per copy $ _____
(please add $2.00 per book for shipping and handling) $ _____
                                                        Total $ _____

_____ Check or _____ Money Order
(Make checks payable to Enlightened Quest Publishing)

_____(____)_____

Name *(Please print)*   Phone

_____

Street *(not P.O. Box)*

_____

City   State   Zip

Send to: **Enlightened Quest Publishing**
Distribution Department
P. O. Box 11692
Birmingham, Alabama 35202

Attention Organizations and Groups:
There are discounts available on bulk purchases of this book
when used for purposes of education, fund raising, etc.